THE LOVE THAT STAYED

EVEN IN SOLITUDE, HER LOVE FOR LIFE NEVER FADED.

KALPITHA R

Made with ♥ on the Notion Press Platform
www.notionpress.com

To those who have ever found peace in their own
company,
To those who have embraced solitude not as emptiness,
but as fulfillment,
And to the ones who have forgotten pieces of themselves
along the way—
May you find the love that has always stayed.

With all my heart,
Kalpitha R

Contents

FOREWORD

There is a quiet kind of strength in solitude—one that is often misunderstood. We live in a world that celebrates connection, companionship, and togetherness, yet there are stories that bloom in the silence of a single presence. The Love That Stayed is one such story.

This book is not about loneliness. It is about choice. It is about a woman who finds fulfillment not in the presence of others, but in the vast, unshaken love she has for her own life. It is about quiet mornings with no expectations, long walks with no destination, and the peace that comes from knowing that one's existence is enough.

But there is always more beneath the surface. As we follow her journey, we begin to ask ourselves: Is solitude truly a decision, or is it sometimes the result of something forgotten?

Through every page, you will find emotions that whisper rather than shout, moments that linger in the spaces between words, and a truth waiting to be uncovered.

So step into her world, feel the weight of her choices, and maybe, just maybe, you will see a reflection of your own story in hers.

— Kalpitha R

PREFACE

Solitude has always fascinated me—not as an emptiness to be feared, but as a space where one can truly exist without expectations. In a world that constantly tells us we need someone, I wanted to write a story about a woman who chooses herself, who loves her life fiercely even when she has no one beside her.

When I first imagined this story, I thought it would simply be about self-love, independence, and the quiet joy of being alone. But as I wrote, I realized that solitude is not always a choice—it can also be a mystery. What if someone loved their life not because they never had anyone, but because they had forgotten that they once did?

The Love That Stayed is about a woman who has built a world of peace around her, yet an unspoken truth lingers in the spaces she does not explore. It is a book about finding completeness within oneself, but it is also about memory, loss, and the invisible ties that connect us to the past.

This story is close to my heart, and I hope it resonates with you. Whether you are someone who cherishes solitude or someone who fears it, I invite you to step into these pages and experience the journey.

Thank you for being here, for reading, and for allowing this story to become a part of you.

ACKNOWLEDGEMENTS

Writing The Love That Stayed has been a deeply personal and emotional journey, and I could not have done it alone.

First and foremost, I am grateful to my parents for their endless love, support, and belief in me. Your encouragement has given me the strength to follow my passion, and for that, I am forever thankful.

To my teachers—Pavithra Ma'am, for guiding me with wisdom and believing in my storytelling; Mau Ma'am, for your encouragement and kind words that have motivated me to keep writing; and Felicit Ma'am, whose support in the beginning helped me take my first steps as a writer. Even though we may not be in touch, I will always be grateful for your influence.

To my readers, thank you for picking up this book. Your support means more than words can express. Every story is incomplete without the hearts that receive it, and I am honored that my words have found their way to you.

And finally, to the stories themselves—the ones I have written and the ones still waiting to be told. May they continue to find their way into the world, touching hearts and inspiring souls.

With gratitude,
Kalpitha R

PROLOGUE

The world wakes up in a quiet hum—soft light spilling through her window, the distant murmur of life moving beyond the walls of her home. But inside, it is still. Peaceful.

She stretches beneath the warmth of her blankets, her body unconcerned with the rush of time. No alarms ring. No footsteps echo from another room. No one calls her name. And yet, she does not grieve this silence. She welcomes it.

For years, she has belonged to no one but herself. No ties, no expectations, no histories binding her to another soul. She has walked through bustling streets unnoticed, dined at candlelit tables alone, and celebrated milestones that no one else remembered. And in all of it, she has found something most people spend their lives searching for—contentment.

She is not lonely. Loneliness is a longing for something that is missing. But she has never felt that absence.

Or so she believes.

Because somewhere, buried beneath the life she has built, beneath the love she has poured into herself, lies a truth she cannot see. A truth the world remembers, but she does not.

And one day, when the silence shifts—when the weight of forgotten memories begins to stir—will she still love the life she thought was hers alone?

A Life of Her Own

I

The Silence She Wakes Up To

The world outside is stirring, but inside, there is nothing but silence. The kind of silence that isn't heavy or hollow—it is whole, like a warm cocoon wrapping around her. No alarm blares beside her bed, no voices echo from another room. The air is still, untouched by the presence of another.

She wakes up not to the sound of a name being called or footsteps shuffling outside her door, but to the gentle hum of morning itself. The soft glow of sunlight trickles in through her half-drawn curtains, spilling golden hues onto the wooden floor. She blinks, slowly adjusting to the world beyond the realm of dreams, stretching her limbs against the coolness of her sheets.

There is no rush.

No one waiting for her.

No urgency to answer to anyone.

She turns to her side and gazes at the empty space beside her. The bed is large enough for two, but it has only ever belonged to her. The pillow remains undisturbed, the blankets unwrinkled except for where she lay. If there is a metaphor for her life, it is this—vast, unshared, yet entirely hers.

A deep breath.

She savors this moment—the stillness before the world demands movement, the weightlessness of existing without expectations.

She throws the covers aside, letting the morning chill brush against her bare skin. The feeling is invigorating, like a reminder that she is alive, and that in itself is enough. She doesn't need a reason to be happy. She doesn't need anyone to validate the life she has built.

The wooden floor creaks beneath her feet as she stands, padding slowly towards the window. She pulls the curtain back fully, allowing the sunlight to drench her in warmth. The city hums beyond her glass pane—cars moving in organized chaos, strangers walking briskly, conversations merging into the melody of an ordinary day. Yet, none of it reaches her in a way that matters.

She is here.

Alone, yet completely content.

She has known loneliness before. The kind that gnaws at your insides, that makes you feel like a shadow walking through a world that does not see you. But this is different. This solitude is hers by choice. It is not a wound. It is not an emptiness to be filled.

It is home.

She turns away from the window and steps into the kitchen, her bare feet pressing against the cold tile. Every plate, every cup, every item in this space belongs to her alone. There is no second mug waiting for someone else. No extra chair that will be pulled out by another. The coffee maker hums as she starts her morning brew, filling the air with the rich scent of familiarity.

She takes her time.

There is no one to rush for, no conversation to force over breakfast. Just the quiet drip of coffee, the soft rustle of the newspaper she barely reads, and the slow, rhythmic beats of her own heart.

She doesn't need noise.

She doesn't need company.

She has herself.

And that is enough.

She wraps her fingers around the warm mug, feeling the heat seep into her palms. The scent of freshly brewed coffee curls into the air, rich and familiar. She doesn't add sugar. She never has. The bitterness feels real, unfiltered—just like the life she has built for herself.

She takes slow sips, savoring the quiet as she leans against the kitchen counter. Outside, the city moves in its endless rhythm, people rushing to their jobs, their families, their responsibilities. She watches through the large window, a silent observer of lives that do not intersect with hers.

There was a time when she thought she needed that—connections, conversations, the comfort of belonging. But now, as she stands here, wrapped in nothing but solitude and the warm embrace of morning light, she knows she belongs to something greater. She belongs to herself.

She moves through her home like a ghost that has claimed its space.

Every object is exactly where she left it. The books on the coffee table remain untouched by anyone but her. The plants by the window lean toward the sun, stretching in quiet companionship. There are no misplaced shoes by the door, no forgotten mugs on the dining table, no signs of another presence.

Her phone remains face down on the counter. No messages, no missed calls. The silence is uninterrupted. She doesn't check it. She never does in the morning.

Some might call it loneliness.

She calls it peace.

The bathroom mirror reflects her face, fresh from sleep, eyes still heavy with dreams she doesn't remember. She brushes her fingers against her cheek, feeling the warmth of her own skin.

She exists.

Not for anyone else. Not to be seen or acknowledged or loved.

She simply exists, and that is enough.

Warm water cascades over her shoulders as she steps into the shower, steam curling around her like an embrace. There is no rush, no need to hurry. The world outside moves at its own frantic pace, but here, in the quiet sanctuary of her home, time stretches endlessly.

She closes her eyes, tilting her head back, letting the water wash over her. This is her moment.

No one calls for her. No one knocks on the door, demanding attention.

The silence follows her, faithful and unwavering.

Dressed in comfortable, oversized clothes, she pads back to the kitchen, where her coffee has cooled but still holds the taste of morning. She picks up a book from the stack on the table and settles into the couch, pulling a blanket over her legs.

She gets lost in the words, the world between the pages. Stories of people who are nothing like her—women who fall in love, men who fight for their dreams, families that break and heal. She has never been part of a story like that.

And she is okay with that.

She doesn't crave romance. She doesn't long for friendships or the laughter of a family filling the empty spaces of her home.

She has carved a life out of solitude, and she wouldn't trade it for anything.

Later, she steps onto her small balcony, the air crisp against her skin. She watches the world move below—children walking to school, lovers holding hands, workers rushing to catch their buses.

She wonders if anyone down there is like her.

Completely alone, yet completely at peace.

She leans against the railing, breathing in the morning air.

A quiet smile tugs at the corner of her lips.

Today is just another day.

And she loves it.

The city hums below her, but she remains untouched by its urgency. She watches, detached yet content, as the world moves on without her. The wind brushes against her skin, cool and gentle, and she closes her eyes for a moment, allowing herself to simply exist.

She lifts her coffee to her lips, now cold, but she drinks it anyway. The bitterness lingers on her tongue, grounding her in the present.

No one knows where she is at this moment.

No one wonders what she's doing.

She could disappear today, and nothing would change.

But that thought doesn't sadden her. If anything, it makes her feel lighter—like she is free in a way most people aren't.

No expectations. No responsibilities. No one waiting for her.

She is not a daughter to be called home, not a friend to be checked on, not a lover to be missed.

She is simply herself.

And that is enough.

She moves back inside, her bare feet silent against the wooden floor. She likes the way her home feels—open, spacious, untouched by chaos. Everything has a place, and nothing is ever out of order.

A single bed in the bedroom.

One chair at the dining table.

A single toothbrush in the holder by the sink.

Nothing is shared. Nothing is borrowed. Nothing is missing.

She wonders, sometimes, what it would be like to have someone else here. Another voice breaking the silence, another presence filling the spaces she so carefully preserves. Would it be warm? Or would it feel suffocating?

She shakes the thought away.

It doesn't matter.

She is happy like this.

She doesn't need to belong to someone else to feel complete.

The day stretches before her, endless and unclaimed.

She eats breakfast slowly, savoring every bite, knowing that no one will judge her for eating alone. The silence isn't empty—it is full of her presence, her thoughts, her small joys.

She waters the plants by the window, watching the droplets soak into the soil. They thrive in her care, just as she thrives in her solitude.

She listens to music, letting the melody wrap around her.

She dances, just because she can.

There is no one to watch.

No one to judge.

No one to share the moment with.

And yet, she smiles.

Because she loves this life.

She loves the simplicity of it, the freedom, the quiet certainty that she is enough.

She doesn't need anyone to tell her that.

She already knows.

As the day fades into evening, she steps onto the balcony again, watching the sky burn into shades of orange and pink.

The world moves on, people returning to homes filled with families, with love, with conversations that spill into the night.

She watches from a distance, but she doesn't feel like she's missing anything.

Her world is smaller, quieter.

But it is hers.

And that is all she has ever wanted.

The sun sinks lower, painting golden streaks across the horizon. She remains on the balcony, watching as the sky melts into darker hues. The warmth of the day lingers in the air, but soon, the coolness of the evening will settle in.

She wraps her arms around herself, not out of loneliness, but simply because it feels nice. The wind plays with her hair, and she closes her eyes, inhaling the scent of the world outside—distant street food stalls, wet earth from a recent drizzle, a faint trace of blooming jasmine carried by the breeze.

For a moment, she imagines a voice calling her name. A soft, familiar voice.

She opens her eyes.

Silence.

Of course.

There is no one.

She steps back inside, shutting the balcony door behind her. The house feels different in the evenings—quieter, heavier in its stillness. Not suffocating, not unwelcome, just... different.

The clock ticks softly, marking the passage of time.

She doesn't feel lonely.

She never feels lonely.

She keeps telling herself that.

She prepares a simple dinner—something warm, something that fills her stomach but not the spaces in her life. The sizzle of vegetables in the pan is the only sound accompanying her. The smell of spices fills the kitchen, curling into the air, yet there is no one to say, That smells good.

She eats at the dining table, where only one chair is pulled out. The other chairs remain neatly tucked in, untouched, unneeded.

Her phone stays where it always does—facedown, silent, forgotten.

She wonders, absently, if anyone thought of her today.

If anyone wondered where she was, what she was doing.

She shakes the thought away.

It doesn't matter.

She doesn't need to be remembered.

After dinner, she washes the dishes, the warm water soothing against her fingers. The act is almost meditative—washing, rinsing, placing each dish back in its place. There is something peaceful about knowing that everything is as it should be.

She walks through her home, turning off the lights one by one. Each room fades into darkness, but nothing feels eerie. Nothing feels empty.

The silence is not a void—it is a presence of its own.

She likes it.

She loves it.

Doesn't she?

In bed, she stares at the ceiling, the fan whirring above her.

The night presses in, wrapping around her like a familiar embrace.

She pulls the blanket up to her chin and lets out a slow breath.

She is alone.

But she is happy.

She has always been happy.

Hasn't she?

Her eyelids grow heavy, her breathing slows, and as she drifts into sleep, a faint, unshakable feeling lingers in the quiet.

A whisper in the back of her mind.

A feeling she cannot name.

Something forgotten.

Something lost.

But sleep takes her before she can think too much about it.

And in the silence, the night watches over her, as it always has.

As it always will.

II

The Echoes She Ignores

The morning arrives the same way it always does—soft, slow, and silent.

She wakes up to the golden light slipping through her curtains, stretching across the floor like a quiet invitation to start the day. She blinks at the ceiling, feeling the weight of sleep still clinging to her limbs.

Another day.

Another morning of stillness.

She doesn't rush to get up. There is no reason to.

The house is waiting, unchanged. The world outside moves at its own frantic pace, but within these walls, time belongs to her.

And yet...

Something feels different today.

She moves through her routine the way she always does.

Brushing her teeth. Showering. Making coffee. The smell fills the air, wrapping around her like an old friend. She drinks it standing by the window, watching the city below.

The streets are alive with movement—cars honking, people talking, children laughing as they run to school. The world is full of noise.

But her world is not.

She takes another sip of coffee, savoring the bitterness.

She should feel at peace.

But today, the silence feels different.

Heavier.

Like something lingers in the spaces between her breaths.

Like something unseen is waiting to be remembered.

She shakes the thought away.

The day passes as it always does—reading, cooking, watering her plants, walking on the balcony, listening to music.

But at times, she catches herself pausing, staring at nothing, feeling an odd sense of déjà vu.

She touches the edge of the dining table and hesitates.

For a second, it feels like a memory flickers at the edges of her mind—something warm, something familiar.

A voice. A laugh.

She blinks, and it's gone.

She frowns.

She never had anyone. She has always been alone.

Hasn't she?

Evening arrives, and with it, the shadows stretch longer, the quiet deepens.

She eats dinner in the same solitary way she always does.

But the silence feels... unnatural tonight.

It clings to her skin, curling around her like something unseen, something forgotten.

She shakes her head, standing up abruptly, her chair scraping against the floor. The sound is loud in the quiet house. Too loud.

She suddenly wants noise. Wants to turn on the TV, play music—something, anything to break this strange feeling pressing against her chest.

But she doesn't.

She takes a deep breath. She is fine.

She has always been fine.

She loves her life.

She loves being alone.

Doesn't she?

That night, as she lies in bed, staring at the ceiling, the feeling does not fade.

Something is missing.

Or perhaps... something has been taken.

She closes her eyes.

And in the darkness, she almost hears it again.

A voice. A whisper.

A name.

Her name.

Spoken not by herself, but by someone else.

Someone who should not exist.

She turns onto her side, pulling the blanket closer, as if that could shield her from the eerie weight pressing against her chest.

It's nothing. Just a trick of the mind.

She has lived alone for as long as she can remember.

There has never been a voice calling her name.

And yet...

Sleep does not come easily.

She stares at the darkness, her breaths slow, measured.

The silence used to feel like home. It used to be comforting.

Tonight, it feels like something else.

Something watching.

Something waiting.

She must have fallen asleep at some point because when she opens her eyes, the room is bathed in early morning light.

For a moment, she feels... strange.

Like waking up from a dream she can't remember.

She sits up, rubbing her temples. There's a dull ache in her head, as if she had been thinking too hard in her sleep.

Shrugging off the unease, she gets out of bed. The floor is cool against her feet as she makes her way to the bathroom.

She flicks on the light.

And then she freezes.

Her toothbrush isn't where she left it.

It's on the other side of the sink.

Her heart stutters for just a second.

She stares at it, unblinking.

A slow chill creeps up her spine.

She lives alone.

No one else has been here.

And yet...

She remembers placing it in its usual spot last night. She always does.

She swallows hard.

Maybe she moved it without realizing it. Maybe she was tired. Maybe she's overthinking.

Yes. That must be it.

She shakes her head, forcing a small smile. "I need to stop scaring myself."

Her voice sounds strange in the quiet.

The day continues as usual, but something lingers at the edges of her awareness.

She feels it in the way her fingers hesitate when she reaches for things, in the way her gaze flickers to corners of the house as if expecting to see something there.

She feels it in the way she moves—more cautious, more aware.

Like she is no longer alone.

Like the silence isn't just silence anymore.

Like it is hiding something.

That evening, she stands by the bookshelf, running her fingers along the spines of books she has read a hundred times.

And then, out of the corner of her eye, she sees it.

The picture frame.

Face down.

Her breath catches.

She never touches that frame.

She never moves it.

With trembling fingers, she reaches for it, slowly turning it over.

Her own face stares back at her.

But she isn't alone in the photo.

There are others.

Smiling faces. Familiar faces.

Faces she cannot name.

A lump rises in her throat.

Her hands tighten around the frame.

Her heart pounds.

Who are they?

Why does she not remember them?

She stumbles back, nearly knocking over a chair.

The silence presses in around her, heavier than ever.

And for the first time in years...

She is afraid.

Her breath comes in shallow gasps as she stares at the photograph.

The people in it—smiling, arms around each other, around her—feel like strangers. But deep inside, something tugs at her.

Something familiar.

She presses a hand to her forehead, the pounding in her skull growing worse.

Who are they?

Why can't she remember?

A rush of panic grips her chest. She flips the frame over again, pressing it down against the shelf as if hiding it will erase the unease crawling under her skin.

Maybe it's an old photo. Maybe she bought it at a thrift store. Maybe it's nothing.

But she knows that's a lie.

She knows this house. Every item in it. Every carefully placed thing.

She has never bought something meaningless.

Everything in this house belongs to her.

So why doesn't this memory?

She backs away from the shelf, her fingers trembling.

She needs air.

She needs to breathe.

The walls feel too close, the silence too thick. It's pressing down on her, swallowing her whole.

She stumbles toward the door, flinging it open. The cool evening air greets her, brushing against her skin, grounding her.

She grips the railing of the balcony, staring down at the moving world below.

Normal. Everything looks normal.

People laughing, cars honking, someone shouting playfully to a friend across the street.

But inside her?

Nothing is normal anymore.

She looks down at her hands.

Her fingers still feel warm from holding the frame.

The weight of it lingers, even though she let it go.

The faces in the photo are gone from her sight.

But they are in her mind now.

Unshakable.

Lingering.

Waiting.

Her grip tightens on the railing.

She doesn't understand.

She doesn't remember.

But for the first time in a long, long time...

She isn't so sure she's been alone at all.

She forces herself to breathe, slow and deep, but the air feels thick, weighted with something unseen.

The city below is alive, people moving, talking, existing in a world she has long kept at a distance.

But inside her?

Inside her, something is breaking.

She closes her eyes, pressing her palms flat against the cold metal of the railing.

Maybe she's just tired. Maybe this is nothing.

Maybe...

Her thoughts cut off as a faint sound drifts through the silence.

A whisper.

So soft she almost thinks she imagined it.

She whirls around, her heart hammering against her ribs.

The apartment is empty.

It always has been.

Hasn't it?

She hesitates before stepping back inside, her body tense, her fingers curled into fists.

The air feels different now.

It's her home. She knows it's her home. Every inch, every corner.

But tonight, it feels unfamiliar.

Or maybe...

Maybe she's the unfamiliar one.

Her eyes flick to the bookshelf. The picture frame still lies face down, exactly where she left it.

She should leave it that way.

Pretend she never saw it.

Go to bed. Forget.

But something inside her won't let her.

Slowly, cautiously, she steps forward.

Her hands tremble as she picks up the frame again.

The photograph is the same.

Her.

And them.

Three people. A woman and two men.

They are smiling.

She is, too.

Her gaze locks onto her own reflection in the image.

She looks... happy.

Her chest tightens.

She doesn't remember ever looking like that.

She doesn't remember them.

And yet, staring at their faces, she feels something deep inside her shift.

A feeling she can't explain.

A loss she never knew she had.

A sharp pain pierces her skull.

She gasps, stumbling back.

The photo frame slips from her fingers, crashing onto the floor.

Glass shatters, scattering across the wooden surface.

Her breath is ragged, uneven.

She clutches her head, squeezing her eyes shut.

Images flash—

A warm hand in hers.

Laughter echoing through a sunlit room.

A voice calling her name.

Her name.

Not just as she knows it.

But as if it belonged to someone else.

As if it belonged to them.

She opens her eyes, panting.

The apartment is silent again.

But it no longer feels empty.

Because now, she knows.

She wasn't always alone.

And the echoes she ignored...

They were never just echoes.

They were memories.

Forgotten.

Or stolen.

III

The Fragments She Cannot Place

She stands frozen, her breath shallow, her heart pounding against her ribs.

Shattered glass glistens on the floor, reflecting fragments of her face.

But the real fracture is inside her.

Something is wrong.

Something has always been wrong.

She thought she loved her solitude. She thought she had chosen this life.

But now... now she isn't sure.

She kneels down slowly, hesitating before picking up the broken frame. Her fingers shake as she carefully lifts the photograph from the shattered glass.

The edges are torn slightly, but the image remains untouched.

Their faces remain untouched.

And something deep inside her stirs.

She takes the photo to the kitchen, placing it on the counter as she fills a glass of water.

Her throat is dry.

Her hands won't stop trembling.

She takes slow sips, forcing herself to breathe, to think.

Who are they?

Why does she not remember them?

Why does looking at their faces feel like she has lost something she never even knew was missing?

Her mind is a maze of questions, but there are no answers.

Only silence.

And yet...

For the first time, she is afraid of that silence.

She carries the photo to the living room, sitting on the couch, tracing a finger over the smiling faces.

They matter.

She knows they do.

But no names come to her. No memories.

Only a hollow ache in her chest.

She flips the photo over.

There is something written on the back.

Her breath catches.

Her own handwriting.

She recognizes the curve of the letters, the slant of the ink.

Happy days, forever together.

A chill runs through her.

She wrote this.

But she doesn't remember ever writing it.

She doesn't remember ever knowing them.

Her fingers tighten around the photo.

This is real.

This is proof that she hasn't always been alone.
That she had someone.
That she lost someone.
But how?
And why?
The apartment suddenly feels too small.
Too quiet.
Too empty.
She needs answers.
She needs to know.
She rushes to her drawers, pulling them open, searching.
There must be more.
More pictures. More proof.
Something. Anything.
But there's nothing.
Only neatly folded clothes, old receipts, and objects she recognizes.
Nothing unfamiliar.
Nothing new.
Nothing except...
She stops.
At the very back of the drawer, buried under layers of fabric, her fingers brush against something smooth.
A book.
No, a journal.
She pulls it out, her breath catching.
It's old. Worn.
But the second she touches it, something inside her sparks.
Familiarity.
Fear.
She flips it open.
The first page is blank.

The second, too.

She turns page after page.

Nothing.

Nothing.

Nothing.

And then—

A single entry.

Scrawled in hurried, desperate handwriting.

If I ever find this...

If I ever start to remember...

Please, don't stop searching.

She stares at the words, her heart in her throat.

It's her handwriting.

Her own message.

A warning.

A plea.

Her fingers tighten around the journal.

Something happened to her.

Something she wasn't supposed to remember.

But now?

Now, she does.

And she won't stop until she uncovers the truth.

No matter what it takes.

The words on the page blur as she stares at them, her breath caught somewhere between disbelief and fear.

If I ever find this...

If I ever start to remember...

Please, don't stop searching.

She rereads the message, tracing the letters with trembling fingers. The ink is slightly smudged, as if it had been written in a hurry, in desperation.

Her heart pounds, each beat echoing in her ears.

She wrote this.

She left this for herself.

But why?

Her hands tighten around the edges of the journal, her knuckles turning white. She flips through the rest of the pages, searching for more, for something—anything—that could explain what this means.

But the rest of the journal is empty.

Blank.

Just this single message, left behind like a whisper from a past she can't remember.

A past someone has stolen from her.

She presses the journal against her chest, squeezing her eyes shut.

The silence of the apartment is suffocating now.

Not comforting.

Not peaceful.

Suffocating.

It has always been hers, this silence. But suddenly, she doesn't know if it's a choice she made or a prison she's been trapped in.

She thought she loved being alone.

She thought this life—this quiet, solitary life—was hers.

But what if it isn't?

What if it never was?

Her mind is racing.

She needs air.

Needs to move.

She pushes herself up, gripping the journal so tightly her fingers ache. The wooden floor creaks under her feet as she walks toward the window, staring out at the city below.

The world outside is still moving.

Still normal.

People walking, cars passing, laughter spilling from somewhere in the distance.

A world full of life.

And yet, hers has been frozen.

Suspended in time.

Or erased.

Her fingers press against the cool glass of the window.

She feels like a ghost.

A shadow of someone she used to be.

But who was she before?

Before this silence.

Before this emptiness.

Before she forgot.

Or was made to forget.

She turns away from the window, her reflection flickering in the glass.

She doesn't recognize herself anymore.

Not truly.

She's been living in a home she thought was hers, following a routine she thought she chose.

But what if she was simply following the echoes of a life she had been left with?

The remains of something bigger, something real, now buried beneath this lonely existence.

She needs to know the truth.

And she will find it.

Even if it shatters everything she thought she knew.

She moves with purpose now, going back to the bookshelf where the photograph still sits.

It is the only proof she has that she wasn't always alone.

The only evidence that there was a before.

She picks it up again, ignoring the sharp sting as a piece of glass pricks her skin. A small drop of blood blooms on her fingertip, vivid red against the cold, lifeless surface of the photo frame.

It feels symbolic.

Like she is touching something real for the first time in years.

Like she is waking up.

Her gaze locks onto the faces in the picture.

The woman on the left—long hair, soft eyes, a warmth in her expression.

The man beside her—slightly taller, a kind smile, his arm slung around her shoulders like it belonged there.

The other man—sharp features, a teasing grin, as if he had just finished saying something meant to make her laugh.

And then, her.

Smiling. Radiant.

Happy.

A version of herself she cannot remember.

Her grip on the frame tightens.

Who were they to her?

Family? Friends?

Why does looking at them make her feel like something is clawing at the edges of her mind, begging to be remembered?

And why does she feel like she has lost them?

Like she has already grieved for them—without even knowing who they are?

The pain in her head returns, sharp and relentless.

She stumbles back, pressing a hand to her temple.

Images flicker.

Faint. Blurred.

A flash of laughter.

A warm embrace.

A voice calling her name—not the name she uses now, but something softer, more real.

The scent of something familiar—tea? Coffee? A warm home?

Then—

The sound of something breaking.

A scream.

Darkness.

The images vanish as quickly as they come.

She gasps, gripping the edge of the table to steady herself.

The pain fades, but the emptiness in her chest remains.

Something happened to her.

Something she was never meant to remember.

And someone—someone—is missing.

No.

Not just someone.

Everyone.

She wasn't always alone.

She had people. A home. A life.

And then...

She lost them.

Or they lost her.

She forces herself to breathe.

She cannot panic.

She cannot break.

She needs to remember.

Her own note—the warning she left herself—rings in her mind.

Don't stop searching.

Her past is hidden from her.

But it is still there.

Buried beneath this silence.

Waiting to be found.

And this time—

She won't ignore the echoes.

She will follow them.

Even if they lead her to a truth she isn't ready for.

Even if it means uncovering something she was never supposed to know.

Because this time...

She will remember.

The weight of the journal is heavy in her hands, as if it carries the pieces of a life she has lost.

Her own handwriting stares back at her.

If I ever find this... If I ever start to remember... Please, don't stop searching.

She should be terrified.

A part of her is terrified.

But stronger than the fear is the undeniable truth pressing against the walls of her mind—she has been living a lie.

Not one she told herself.

One that was given to her.

One that was forced upon her.

And she needs to know why.

The air in the apartment is still, suffocating, too quiet.

Her breath is shallow as she flips through the journal again, hoping for more.

Something.

Anything.

But there's nothing.

No dates. No other messages.

Just that single warning.

It feels like a voice from a different version of herself—one that was desperate to remember.

One that left this behind because she knew someday, she would need it.

And now, that day has come.

She sets the journal down, pressing her hands against the wooden table, grounding herself.

If she left herself a message, it means she knew something was wrong.

It means she must have started remembering before.

But why did she stop?

Did she give up?

Or was she made to forget again?

A shiver runs down her spine.

The thought is horrifying.

The idea that someone might have erased her past—twice—fills her with a terror unlike anything she has ever known.

But she clenches her fists.

No.

She won't let it happen again.

Not this time.

She needs answers.

And she won't stop until she finds them.

Her gaze drifts back to the photograph.

It still lies there on the table, untouched.

The three people in it—smiling, alive, hers.

And yet, nameless.

Forgotten.

She picks it up, staring at their faces, searching for something familiar.

It's strange.

She doesn't remember them.

But she feels them.

A warmth in her chest.

A quiet ache, like a song she used to know but can no longer hum.

She traces the woman's face with her fingertip.

Is she... her mother?

A sister?

She looks kind. Gentle.

Someone who might have held her when she cried.

Someone who might have loved her.

And the man beside her?

The easy smile. The way he leans in like he belongs.

A friend? A brother?

Or something more?

Her heart tightens at the thought.

And the third—

His grin is sharp, playful, like he's about to say something that would make her roll her eyes and laugh anyway.

Her throat closes.

She knows them.

Even if she doesn't remember them, she knows them.

They were hers.

They are hers.

And she lost them.

Or they lost her.

She places the photo down carefully, her fingers lingering over it.

She needs to find out who they are.

Who she was.

And there's only one place to start.

Her home.

The very walls around her.

Because if there's one hidden truth, there may be more.

She moves through the apartment, her footsteps slow and measured.

The air feels different now.

Like it isn't hers anymore.

Like it never was.

Her fingers trail along the bookshelves, the kitchen counter, the framed artwork on the walls.

All things she recognizes.

Things she thought belonged to her.

But now, she wonders.

Did she choose them?

Or did someone put them here to make her believe this was her life?

The thought sends a chill down her spine.

She moves to the bedroom, pulling open drawers, searching.

But everything is ordinary.

Familiar.

Nothing out of place.

Until—

She pauses.

The closet door.

It's shut, like always.

But suddenly, she feels uneasy looking at it.

She swallows hard.

It's just a closet.

It should be just a closet.

But her body feels tense, her breath shallow.

Like she already knows she's about to find something she won't be able to ignore.

Her hand shakes as she reaches for the handle.

And then—

She pulls it open.

At first, it looks normal.
Clothes. Shoes. Boxes on the top shelf.
But then—
Her eyes land on something shoved into the corner.
A small, locked suitcase.
She doesn't own a suitcase.
At least, she doesn't remember owning one.
Her pulse quickens.
She crouches, running her fingers along the lock.
There's no key in sight.
But she's not about to stop now.
She grabs a bobby pin from the dresser, her fingers working quickly, clumsily.
Her heart pounds.
Click.
Click.
Then—
A sharp snap.
The lock pops open.
Her breath catches.
She hesitates only for a second.
And then she lifts the lid.
Inside, there are papers.
Stacks of them.
Some are yellowed with age. Others look newer.
She picks one up, her hands trembling.
And then she freezes.
It's a birth certificate.
Her birth certificate.
But the name printed on it—
It isn't hers.
Or at least, it isn't the name she knows as hers.
Her vision blurs.

She shuffles through more documents, scanning them frantically.

Medical records. School forms.

Each one with a name that is both hers and not hers.

And then—

Her breath stops.

A newspaper clipping, creased and fragile.

She smooths it out, her eyes darting across the words.

And what she reads makes her blood run cold.

"Young Woman Goes Missing—Family Desperate for Answers."

A photo accompanies the article.

A photo of her.

But below it, the names of the people searching for her—

The same names that were lost to her.

The same faces in the photograph she found.

A family she was never meant to remember.

A past she was never meant to find.

And the horrifying truth—

She didn't lose them.

They lost her.

Someone took her away.

Someone erased her.

And whoever did it...

They might still be watching.

IV

The Life She Was Stolen From

The newspaper trembles in her hands.

The words blur, not because of the faded ink, but because of the storm brewing behind her eyes.

"Young Woman Goes Missing—Family Desperate for Answers."

The article is old. The edges worn, the paper delicate between her fingers.

She reads it again. And again.

And then once more, until the truth is carved into her mind.

This isn't just a story.

It's her story.

She wasn't just lost.

She was taken.

And the people in the photograph—

The ones who have haunted her dreams, the ones whose smiles felt like ghosts of a life she couldn't reach—

They are her family.

Her real family.

And they have been looking for her.

Her breath comes in short gasps.

She presses her palm against the cold floor, steadying herself.

The room spins.

Her mind spins.

The life she built—the life she thought she loved—shatters in a heartbeat.

She was never meant to be alone.

She was never meant to wake up in silence every morning, thinking it was hers.

She had people.

She had love.

And somehow, all of it was ripped away from her.

But how?

And why?

Her fingers curl around the newspaper, crumpling the edges.

Who did this to me?

Her heart pounds, a mix of rage and fear clawing at her chest.

Because if she was taken...

If she was erased from the lives of the people who loved her...

Then someone wanted her to forget.

Someone made sure she wouldn't remember.

And now that she has started remembering—

What if they come back to stop her?

Her pulse is erratic as she stumbles back, pushing the suitcase away as if it burns to touch it.

She can't stay here.

Not anymore.

This apartment—this life—it was never hers.

It was a prison.

A carefully constructed illusion.

And now that she has torn through the curtain, she knows she can never unsee the truth.

Someone built this life for her.

Someone placed her here.

And that same someone could be watching.

She grabs the journal—the one she left for herself.

The words on the page are seared into her mind.

"Please, don't stop searching."

She won't.

She can't.

She shoves the newspaper into her pocket, along with the photograph, her hands moving quickly now.

She needs to find them.

The people in the picture.

The people who once called her theirs.

She doesn't know if they still live in the same place, if they ever gave up searching for her, if they moved on—

If they even believe she is alive.

But she has to try.

Because if she was taken, that means someone has answers.

And she won't stop until she finds them.

Even if it means confronting the person who stole her life.

As she steps toward the door, a sudden, sharp noise cuts through the silence.

A footstep.

Outside.

Right by her door.

She freezes.
The air turns thick, heavy.
Her fingers tighten around the edge of the suitcase.
The apartment was always quiet.
Always still.
No one ever came to visit.
No one ever knocked.
But now—
A shadow shifts beneath the door.
A presence she cannot see but can feel.
And then, a whisper.
Low. Faint.
But unmistakable.
"She knows."
Her breath catches in her throat.
A chill races down her spine.
And in that moment, she knows—
She is not safe.
Not here.
Not anymore.
Someone is watching.
Someone knows.
And they aren't going to let her leave.
The whisper lingers in the air like a ghost.
"She knows."
The weight of those two words crushes her chest, making it impossible to breathe.
Someone is out there.
Someone who has been watching her.
And now they know—
She is starting to remember.
Her heart slams against her ribs as her mind spirals into a thousand terrifying possibilities.

Who are they?

How long have they been keeping her here?

What will they do now that she has figured it out?

A part of her wants to believe she imagined it.

That the fear, the overwhelming shock of everything she has uncovered, is making her paranoid.

But she knows what she heard.

She felt the presence outside that door.

And the truth is suffocating—

She is not alone.

She never was.

The floor beneath her feels unsteady as she takes a step back, her legs shaking.

Her mind screams at her to run, to leave everything behind and get out.

But where?

Where would I even go?

The people in the photograph—her family—she doesn't even know where they are.

And whoever did this to her... they have been in control all this time.

They took her. They erased her.

And they will not let her walk away so easily.

She swallows hard, forcing her breath to steady.

Think.

Don't panic.

She has spent years believing she was alone, but now she knows—someone put her here.

That means they must have kept some kind of record.

Something that proves what they did to her.

Something that can help her escape.

Her eyes dart back to the suitcase.

She crouches, digging through the files with trembling hands, flipping through pages she doesn't fully understand.

Medical records.

Psychiatric evaluations.

Handwritten notes.

She pauses.

A letter.

One that seems more personal, folded neatly as if someone took great care in placing it here.

Her breath shudders as she opens it.

Patient Report – Subject 314

Status: Successfully relocated.

Memory suppression: Holding steady. No recall episodes recorded in the past 12 months.

Recommendation: Continue monitoring. Reintegration remains impossible without risk.

Her stomach turns violently.

Memory suppression.

They did something to her.

She was never alone by choice.

She was never meant to remember.

A sickening realization crashes over her.

She didn't just lose her family.

She didn't just forget them.

They were stolen from her.

Erased.

And someone—whoever wrote this—was making sure she never got them back.

Her fingers tighten around the paper.

Her entire life, she thought she was free.

She thought she was choosing to live in solitude.

But it was never her choice.

It was a cage.

A beautifully crafted, silent prison.

And now—

Now, she has broken free.

A sudden, soft creak outside the door sends ice through her veins.

The whisper wasn't her imagination.

Someone is still there.

Still listening.

Still waiting.

Her body goes rigid as her mind flashes through every possibility.

She doesn't know who they are.

She doesn't know how much danger she's in.

But she knows one thing—

She cannot let them know that she has read this.

Her fingers move quickly, stuffing the papers back into the suitcase, locking it again as quietly as she can.

She forces her breaths to slow, to steady.

If they know she has figured it out, they might come inside.

They might take her away again.

She stands, pressing herself against the wall, listening.

Silence.

Then, the softest sound—

A single, slow step retreating from her door.

She counts.

One.

Two.

Three.

Then nothing.

Whoever was there...

They're gone.

For now.

She doesn't move for a long time.

Minutes pass, or maybe hours.

Time feels slippery, unreal.

She only knows one thing—

She needs to leave.

She needs to get out of here before they come back.

Before they make her forget again.

Because if they have done it once—

What's stopping them from doing it again?

Her gaze flickers to the window.

It's not high.

The alley below is empty, dimly lit by the flickering streetlamp.

She doesn't have time to think about whether it's safe.

She doesn't have time to hesitate.

She grabs the photograph, the newspaper, and the letter, shoving them into her jacket.

The rest can stay.

She won't need it anymore.

She will never come back here.

Her fingers push open the window, the night air rushing in, cool against her overheated skin.

She swings one leg over the ledge.

Then the other.

The street below feels like a different world.

One she was never meant to return to.

But she's done living in a lie.

She's done being their experiment.

Their stolen girl.

Their ghost.

She takes one last breath—

And jumps.

The impact rattles her bones, but she doesn't stop.

Her feet hit the pavement, and she runs.
She doesn't know where she's going.
She doesn't know who she can trust.
But she knows one thing—
She will find them.
The people in the photograph.
The ones she lost.
The ones who lost her.
And when she does, she will get back everything they stole from her.
No matter what it takes.

V

No Birthdays, No Celebrations

Her birthday passes like any other day.

No candles. No cake. No messages.

No one remembers.

Because no one knows.

Not even her.

She sits by the window of a small, unfamiliar motel room, staring out at the unfamiliar city.

The neon lights flicker, bleeding color into the night, but they don't reach her.

A cup of tea sits untouched on the table, steam curling into the air.

She doesn't know why she ordered it. She doesn't even like tea.

Or maybe she does.

Maybe she once loved it.

Maybe there was a time when someone—her mother, her sister, someone—would make it for her, handing her a warm cup with a smile, saying, Happy Birthday.

But no memories come.

Nothing except a hollow ache in her chest, a whisper of something lost.

Something stolen.

She had checked the date on the motel calendar that morning.

March 14th.

It meant nothing to her.

A random number. A random day.

Until she found her old identification card, buried beneath the newspaper article in her jacket pocket.

She almost didn't look.

Almost didn't want to know.

But her hands moved on their own, unfolding the worn plastic, eyes scanning the details that should have been hers.

Name: Unknown.

Date of Birth: March 14th.

Blood rushed to her ears.

She had spent years not knowing.

Not caring.

But now, it felt like a slap.

Like something cruel.

How many birthdays had passed unnoticed?

How many times had she woken up, gone about her day, believing it was just another date?

While out there, somewhere, the people in that photograph—her family—were remembering.

Were missing her.

Were maybe even lighting a candle for someone who never came home.

She turns her gaze to the motel mirror, but she barely recognizes herself.

Who is this girl?

This girl with tired eyes, dark circles carved beneath them.

This girl with a face that should have been familiar but feels like a stranger's.

This girl who has lived years believing she chose this life—when in reality, it was given to her.

No.

Not given.

Forced.

Stolen.

She grips the edge of the table, fingers digging into the wood.

She refuses to let them take anything more from her.

They stole her memories.

They stole her life.

They will not steal her future.

She pulls out the old photograph again.

The one with the faces she doesn't remember but feels deep in her bones.

A mother. A father. A sister.

Their arms are around her, holding her close, as if they never wanted to let go.

But someone made them.

Someone took her away, wiped her existence clean from their world.

And she needs to know why.

She needs to know who.

And more than anything—

She needs to go home.

The tea has gone cold by the time she moves again.

She takes a deep breath, reaches for the pen by the bedside, and pulls the motel notepad toward her.

Her hands shake, but she forces herself to write.

Her name—her real name—is still missing from her memory.

Her past is a locked door, the key buried somewhere she can't reach.

But this?

This is something she can control.

She presses the tip of the pen to the paper, writing the only promise that matters.

"Next year, I will not be alone."

"Next year, I will celebrate with them."

She stares at the words, heart pounding.

Then, beneath them, she writes something else.

Something even more important.

"Next year, they will remember me."

And this time—

She will remember them, too.

The motel room is silent except for the ticking of the old clock above the door.

Each second stretches endlessly, pulling her deeper into the weight of what today means.

March 14th.

Her birthday.

And no one knows.

No calls. No texts. No messages from friends or family.

Not because they forgot—

But because, in their world, she does not exist.

The thought sends a shiver down her spine.

How many times had she woken up on this very date, oblivious to the significance of it?

How many times had she let the day pass by without realizing it was meant to be hers?

She wraps her arms around herself, staring at the old photograph once more.

Their faces are blurred at the edges, the ink fading with time, but their emotions remain vivid.

Love. Warmth. Belonging.

Things she has never known.

Or rather—things she once had but was forced to forget.

The air in the room feels suffocating, thick with emotions she can't untangle.

She pushes off the bed, her bare feet touching the cold floor as she moves toward the mirror.

The reflection staring back at her is both familiar and foreign.

She traces her fingers over her cheek, as if searching for something—some proof that this is really her.

Whoever she used to be, whoever they took from that family...

She is nothing like that girl anymore.

She doesn't know what she liked, what made her laugh, what her favorite cake was, if she even liked celebrating birthdays at all.

Did her mother bake her something sweet every year?

Did her father wrap presents with shaky hands, pretending he wasn't terrible at it?

Did her sister barge into her room at midnight, demanding to be the first to say Happy Birthday?

She grips the edge of the sink, breathing hard.

There are no answers in the mirror.

Only more questions.

Only a girl who should have been someone—

But was reduced to no one.

She turns away abruptly, crossing the room and grabbing her coat.

She needs air.

Needs something to remind her she is still here.

That she is still real.

The motel door creaks as she steps outside. The streets are quiet, the world softened by the glow of distant streetlights.

She pulls her coat tighter around herself and starts walking.

No destination. No plan.

Just the rhythm of her footsteps against the pavement, grounding her, pulling her away from the storm inside her head.

Her fingers slip into her pocket, finding the newspaper clipping again.

"Young Woman Goes Missing—Family Desperate for Answers."

She rereads it, even though she already knows every word by heart.

She has spent years living in the comfort of solitude, convincing herself she was free.

That she was happy.

But the truth is clear now—

She was never alone.

She was just forgotten.

And if she doesn't do something soon, she will stay forgotten.

She stops by a small café, its warm light spilling onto the sidewalk.

Through the window, she sees a family—parents and a little girl, huddled together over a cake, laughter bursting in soft waves.

The mother claps as the girl blows out the candles.

The father ruffles her hair.

The girl looks up at them with the kind of love that only comes from knowing—truly knowing—that she belongs.

The scene is so simple, so normal.

Yet it slices through her like a blade.

She used to have this.

She knows it, deep in her bones.

She was someone's daughter.

Someone's sister.

She was loved once.

And now?

She is just a ghost, watching from the outside.

She turns away, blinking fast.

Tears threaten to spill, but she refuses to cry.

Not here.

Not now.

She takes a deep breath, steadying herself.

Then, with a renewed sense of determination, she pulls out the notepad from her jacket pocket.

Her fingers shake as she flips to the page where she made her promise earlier.

"Next year, I will not be alone."

The words stare back at her, solid and certain.

She won't let this birthday be like all the others.

She won't let the people who stole her life keep winning.

She won't let another year pass as a nameless, forgotten girl.

Because she is someone.

She had a family.

And no matter what it takes, no matter how long it takes—

She is going to find them.

She will bring herself back into their lives.

And next year?

Next year, when March 14th comes again—

She will be home.

The cold night air clings to her skin as she walks aimlessly down the empty streets. She doesn't know where she's going—only that she can't stand still. Not tonight. Not when her mind is tangled in a past she doesn't remember.

Her birthday.

A day that should have been filled with warmth, voices, laughter. But there's nothing. Just an unbearable silence that stretches through the years, swallowing every memory, leaving her with a name she doesn't fully recognize and a history she can't piece together.

She shoves her hands into her coat pockets, fingers brushing against the worn newspaper clipping.

The headline is burned into her mind:

"Young Woman Goes Missing—Family Desperate for Answers."

It should feel like a story about someone else. But it doesn't.

It feels like her.

She stops walking, leaning against the rusted railing of a deserted bridge. The water below is dark and restless, reflecting the scattered city lights.

She exhales slowly, watching the breath curl into the air.

"Somewhere out there... they're still waiting for me."

The thought should bring her comfort, but it doesn't. Because if they were waiting—if they were searching—why hasn't she found them yet?

Why hasn't anyone come for her?

The answer lingers at the edges of her mind, too painful to confront.

Maybe they have moved on.

Maybe they stopped searching.

Maybe they don't remember her either.

Her stomach twists. The thought is unbearable, but after everything she's learned, it's possible.

Whoever erased her life did more than just take her away.

They made sure no one could find her.

And if they could do that to her—

What's stopping them from doing it to her family too?

A chill runs down her spine.

She can't think like that. Not yet. Not when she's just starting to uncover the truth.

She needs to focus on what she does know.

The newspaper article is proof that once—years ago—her family fought to bring her home.

She needs to believe that somewhere, in some part of their hearts, they're still waiting.

Still hoping.

And if they've forgotten her, if their memories have been stolen just like hers—

Then she will make them remember.

Her fingers curl around the railing, her resolve hardening.

She won't waste another year being a ghost.

She won't let another birthday pass by unnoticed.

This will be the last one she spends alone.

She glances down at the notepad in her hands, reading the words she wrote earlier:

"Next year, I will not be alone."

"Next year, I will celebrate with them."

"Next year, they will remember me."

She takes a deep breath, then flips the page, pressing the pen against the paper with new determination.

"Tomorrow, I begin."

She doesn't know exactly where to start.

She has no map, no instructions, no clear path forward.

But she has a name.

She has a date.

And somewhere, buried beneath years of erasure and silence—

She has a family.

And she is going to find them.

No matter what it takes.

VI

Love Stories That Are Not Hers

Love is everywhere.

In the way an old man holds the door open for his wife, his hands steady despite his age.

In the way a mother brushes the crumbs off her child's cheeks, her touch tender and automatic.

In the way two strangers laugh over coffee, shoulders inching closer, lost in a world of their own.

She watches them from a distance, unnoticed.

Always unnoticed.

Always outside, looking in.

She sits at the corner of a small café, tucked behind the large glass window, where the world unfolds like a silent movie.

A young couple sits by the fountain across the street, their hands intertwined, their smiles soft. They speak in hushed voices, lost in a universe where no one else exists.

She wonders what it feels like—to be someone's person.

To be someone people wait for, someone who is missed when they're gone.

She wonders if she had that once.

If there was ever a time when someone looked at her the way that boy looks at the girl across from him—like she was the only thing that mattered.

Her fingers tighten around her cup. The warmth of the tea doesn't reach her heart.

It never does.

Because no one looks at her like that.

No one is searching for her in a crowd, waiting at a café, reaching for her hand.

She is just a shadow, passing through unnoticed.

A ghost in a world full of love stories that do not belong to her.

She steps out of the café, the bell above the door jingling softly.

The streets are alive with the quiet hum of the morning.

A child tugs at his father's coat, pointing excitedly at something in a shop window. The father laughs, ruffling the boy's hair before kneeling down to listen, as if his son's words are the most important thing in the world.

A group of friends huddle together, arms slung over each other's shoulders, their conversation spilling into laughter that echoes through the street.

An elderly couple walks hand in hand, their pace slow but steady, as if time itself cannot touch them.

Love exists in so many forms.

Not just in whispered confessions and lingering touches.

Not just in grand gestures and promises of forever.

But in the little things.

The way someone remembers how you like your coffee.

The way a friend stays up late just to talk.

The way a mother hums a song while making breakfast, even if no one is listening.

She understands this.

She sees it everywhere.

But she feels none of it.

Because love is something she has spent years watching from the outside.

Never stepping in.

Never belonging.

The sun is higher now, casting light over the city, filling the streets with warmth.

She wonders if love is like that, too.

Something you can see.

Something you can almost feel.

But never quite touch.

Maybe she was meant to be like this—someone who watches, but never receives.

Maybe she was never meant to have a love story of her own.

Maybe she was never meant to be remembered.

The thought clenches at her chest, but she shoves it away.

No.

Not this time.

She spent years believing she was alone because she chose to be.

But she knows the truth now.

She had love once.

She had people.

And someone took them away from her.

Or worse—took her away from them.

Love once belonged to her, and she refuses to let it slip through her fingers again.

She will find her family.

She will find her place in the world.

And next time, when she watches love from a distance—

She will not be on the outside.

She will be in it.

Right where she belongs.

The sun climbs higher, stretching golden fingers over the streets, warming the world that doesn't see her.

She keeps walking, not sure where she's going—only that she needs to keep moving.

Because stopping means thinking.

And thinking means remembering.

And remembering means pain.

She passes a bookstore, its window display filled with romance novels—love stories told in delicate words, their endings neatly tied with hope.

She stops, staring at the covers.

Lovers frozen in mid-spin, eyes locked as if the world outside their embrace didn't exist.

Hands reaching across time, across space, across every obstacle ever placed between them.

A quiet ache spreads through her.

She wants to scoff at it, to brush it off as fiction.

But deep down, she knows love isn't just something in books.

It's real.

She's seen it, felt the edges of it brushing against her life—always near, but never quite hers.

Always something to observe.

Never something to hold.

She wonders if anyone ever loved her like that.

If someone once held her face in their hands, whispering promises she's long forgotten.

If someone once searched for her in a crowd, eyes lighting up the moment they found her.

If someone once missed her.

Her throat tightens.

No one misses her now.

She is just a shadow.

A girl who existed, once—

And then didn't.

A gust of wind rushes past her, carrying laughter from across the street.

She turns her head, watching as a man kneels in front of a woman, pulling a small velvet box from his pocket.

Gasps ripple through the crowd. The woman's hands fly to her mouth, eyes wide, tears forming.

The man says something—soft, heartfelt, meant only for her ears.

And then, as if she has been waiting her whole life for this moment—

She nods.

The crowd erupts into cheers as she throws her arms around him, kissing him, as if sealing a promise that was always meant to be.

A life together.

A love that chose to stay.

She watches, frozen.

Not because she envies them—

But because something in her chest hurts.

Not a sharp, stabbing pain.

Not jealousy.

But something deeper.

A quiet longing.

A question that whispers through her like a ghost.

"Have I ever been loved like that?"

"And if I was—why did I lose it?"

The moment ends. The couple disappears into the crowd, surrounded by claps, cheers, and warmth.

She remains standing there, alone, unnoticed, as if she was never part of the scene at all.

Just a passerby.

Just an observer.

Watching love happen to everyone but her.

She turns away, forcing her feet to move again.

She doesn't know where she's going.

But she knows one thing—

She is tired of watching.

Tired of existing in the space between belonging and being forgotten.

Tired of being the girl who was erased.

If love was once hers, if she was once someone's sister, daughter, friend—

Then she will find them.

She will bring herself back.

She will be remembered.

And next time—

Next time she sees love, she won't just be a stranger in the background.

She will be part of it.

No longer a ghost.

No longer invisible.

But real.

And this time—

This time, it will be a love story that belongs to her.

VII
Writing Letters to Herself

The world outside moves in a steady rhythm—cars passing, voices drifting through open windows, people filling spaces with their lives. But inside her apartment, everything is still.

No voices. No footsteps. No reminders that she belongs to someone.

Just her.

And the quiet.

She stands in the middle of the small living room, staring at the stack of papers on the coffee table. Blank pages, waiting for her to give them meaning.

A sigh escapes her lips as she sits down, fingers brushing over the smooth surface of the first page.

She has spent years watching—watching love, watching life, watching the world move around her while she remained untouched.

But today, she won't watch.

Today, she will speak.

Even if the only person listening is herself.

She picks up the pen.

For a moment, she hesitates, the weight of silence pressing against her.

But then she exhales slowly, letting the ink flow.

Dear Me,

I know you feel invisible. I know you wonder if anyone remembers you, if anyone misses you, if you were ever meant to belong.

But you exist.

You matter.

You are not a ghost.

You are flesh and bone, dreams and memories, laughter and sorrow.

And you do not need the world to love you to be real.

You are enough.

She stops, her hand trembling slightly.

She lets the words settle before moving to another sheet of paper.

This one, she folds into a small square and tucks into the pocket of her coat.

She will carry it with her. A reminder. A quiet promise.

Because love isn't just something she has lost.

It is something she can give herself.

By the time the afternoon light spills through her window, she has scattered pieces of herself throughout the apartment.

A note on the bathroom mirror:

"You are more than your reflection."

A note by her bedside table:

"You deserve kindness—even from yourself."

A note taped to the fridge:

"Eat. Breathe. Live. You are here."

And on the front door, where she will see it every time she leaves:

"Come back home. You belong here."

Her heart feels lighter.

Maybe she doesn't have a family waiting for her.

Maybe she isn't sure who she used to be.

But today, she is someone.

And that is enough.

For now.

That night, as she lays in bed, she runs her fingers over one last note she had written and placed under her pillow.

The words are simple, but they are the truth.

"You are not alone. You never were."

She closes her eyes, holding onto the promise.

Tomorrow, she will keep searching.

Tomorrow, she will uncover more of herself.

But tonight—

Tonight, she lets herself be loved.

Even if the love only comes from her own hands.

And for the first time in a long time—

That is enough.

The city outside her window hums with life, but inside, there is only the quiet rustling of paper.

She moves slowly through her apartment, finding spaces for her words.

A note beneath the lamp on her nightstand.

A slip of paper tucked inside her favorite book.

A small reminder taped to the inside of her closet door, where she will see it every morning.

Each one carries a piece of her—thoughts she cannot say aloud, love she does not know how to receive from others but is learning to give herself.

She stops by the window, watching the streets below.

The world moves on, unaware of her small act of defiance—of survival.

But it doesn't matter.

Because she knows.

And for the first time, that is enough.

She lingers by the kitchen counter, staring at a blank envelope.

This one is different.

This one is not a note to be left around her home.

This one is a letter—to herself, to the girl she was, to the girl she is trying to become.

She picks up the pen, hesitating only for a second before she begins.

Dear Me,

I know you feel lost. I know you feel like a puzzle with missing pieces, like a book with pages torn out.

But I promise you—your story is still whole.

Even with the gaps, even with the things you cannot remember, you are not empty.

You are here. You are breathing. You are real.

And you do not need someone else to tell you that to believe it.

She pauses, pressing the pen against her lips.

The next words come slowly, carefully.

You are worthy of love. Even if no one says it. Even if no one shows it. Even if you have forgotten what it feels like.

She exhales, folding the letter neatly and slipping it into the envelope.

This one, she will not leave anywhere.

This one, she will keep.

A reminder. A promise.

A piece of herself that cannot be lost.

The sky outside darkens, the streetlights flickering on one by one.

She moves through her apartment, reading each note she has placed.

Soft whispers from her own heart.

Words that she needs to believe.

She touches them lightly, as if pressing them into her skin, into her soul.

And when she reaches her front door, she runs her fingers over the final note—the one that will greet her every time she leaves, every time she returns.

"Come back home. You belong here."

Something tightens in her chest.

She swallows hard, pressing her forehead against the door.

She wants to believe it.

She will believe it.

Because if she doesn't—who else will?

And so, in the quiet of her apartment, in the quiet of her heart, she makes a decision.

She will not disappear.

She will not let herself be forgotten.

She will fight for her place in the world.

And no matter what the truth holds—

She will come back home.

Wherever that may be.

The night air is cool against her skin as she sits by the open window, her fingers brushing over the edges of the letter she just wrote.

It feels strange—comforting, yet heavy—to see her own thoughts laid bare in ink.

She has spent years filling the silence with distractions, with routines that keep her from lingering too long on the ache in her chest.

But now, as she reads her own words, she cannot escape the truth.

She has been waiting.

Waiting for someone to see her.

Waiting for someone to remember her.

Waiting for love to find her.

But maybe... maybe she has been looking in the wrong place.

Maybe love isn't something she has to wait for.

Maybe it's something she can build.

She rises from the chair, pacing through her small apartment, her gaze sweeping over the scattered notes.

The words feel alive, pulsing with quiet reassurance.

But a thought gnaws at the edges of her mind.

What happens when the ink fades?

What happens when these papers crumple, when the glue weakens, when time erases these reminders?

Will she forget? Will she go back to being nothing?

She swallows hard, gripping the edge of the table.

No.

She cannot let that happen.

This love—the one she is learning to give herself—needs to be more than just words on paper.

It needs to be something she carries inside her.

Something she becomes.

A slow breath fills her lungs.

She steps toward the mirror.

Her reflection stares back, quiet, expectant.

She doesn't flinch away this time.

Instead, she reaches out, pressing her palm against the glass as if she can touch the girl on the other side.

For years, she has felt like a ghost.

Like someone who exists on the edges of life, always watching, never belonging.

But in this moment, she sees herself.

And she speaks.

Soft. Certain. Unwavering.

"You are enough."

The words hang in the air.

She repeats them.

Louder this time.

"You are enough."

Again.

"You are enough."

Her voice does not shake.

She does not look away.

Because for the first time in a long time, she believes it.

That night, she does something she hasn't done in years.

She pulls out an old notebook from the back of her closet—one she had bought ages ago but never found the courage to use.

On the first page, she writes:

"This is my story."

Not a story of loss.

Not a story of loneliness.

Not a story of being forgotten.

But a story of becoming.

Of choosing herself, again and again, no matter how many times the world tried to erase her.

She writes until her fingers ache, until the sky outside begins to lighten.

And when she finally closes the book, she does not feel empty.

She feels full.

Full of words.
Full of purpose.
Full of herself.

And for the first time, that is enough.

As she crawls into bed, slipping the last note under her pillow, she lets herself believe—

That even if she has no one, she still has herself.

That even if no one remembers her, she is still here.

And that is something no one can take away.

She closes her eyes, holding onto the quiet love she has built for herself.

A love that will not fade.

A love that will stay.

And with that thought, she finally sleeps.

The Art of Being Enough

VIII

The Freedom of Waking Up Alone

The first thing she notices when she wakes up is the silence.

Not the heavy, aching kind of silence that used to make her chest feel hollow.

This is different.

It is light.

Comfortable.

A kind of silence that belongs to her.

She stretches beneath the covers, feeling the warmth of her own bed wrap around her.

No alarms blaring.

No one calling her name.

No rush to be anywhere but here.

She closes her eyes for a moment, savoring the weightlessness of it.

There was a time when waking up alone felt like a reminder of everything she had lost.

Now, it feels like freedom.

She rolls onto her side, eyes drifting toward the small stack of notes she left on her nightstand the night before.

Her own words greet her, soft and steady.

"You are enough."

"You are here."

"You belong."

She smiles.

The version of herself from yesterday was kind.

She thinks the version of herself today will be, too.

She swings her legs over the edge of the bed and pads barefoot to the kitchen, moving at her own pace.

No hurried footsteps.

No whispered complaints about being late.

No one else's schedule dictating hers.

Just the quiet hum of the morning, and the knowledge that she can take her time.

She puts the kettle on and watches as the steam curls into the air.

She doesn't have to make coffee for someone else.

She doesn't have to wait for a roommate to finish using the bathroom.

She doesn't have to share her favorite mug, the one with tiny stars printed across it.

Everything in this space is hers.

Everything she does is her choice.

She lifts the warm mug to her lips, letting the first sip settle deep in her chest.

It tastes like comfort.

It tastes like herself.

She steps onto the balcony, feeling the cool breeze against her skin.

Below, the city is already awake—cars weaving through streets, people moving with purpose.

She used to wonder where she fit in all of it.

If she was supposed to be out there, tangled in the rush.

If she was missing something by choosing to stay here, in the quiet.

But today, she doesn't wonder.

She doesn't need to.

She likes the way she moves through the world now—unrushed, unbothered, unchained.

She likes that she doesn't have to answer to anyone but herself.

She likes that the only voice shaping her day is her own.

There is something powerful in that.

Something beautiful.

Something that feels like belonging.

She spends the rest of the morning exactly as she wants.

She reads without checking the time.

She eats breakfast slowly, enjoying every bite.

She writes a new letter to herself, not because she needs to, but because she wants to.

And when she catches her reflection in the hallway mirror, she doesn't look away.

She meets her own gaze.

And for the first time, she doesn't see someone waiting for love.

She sees someone whole.

Someone who is enough, just as she is.

Someone who wakes up alone, but never lonely.

And that is a kind of love she never expected to find.

A love that doesn't leave.

A love that stays.

She lingers on the balcony, her fingers wrapped around the warm ceramic of her mug. The sky is still soft with morning light, the air tinged with the scent of rain from the night before. Below, the world moves at its usual hurried pace—cars honking, voices blending into a distant hum, people rushing toward their routines.

But she doesn't have to rush.

She has nowhere to be.

No one waiting for her.

No expectations pulling her in a direction she doesn't want to go.

And for once, that thought doesn't ache.

It soothes.

She closes her eyes, letting the morning breeze dance across her skin.

There was a time when waking up alone felt like a reminder of everything she had lost.

A weight.

A punishment.

She used to wake up and reach for someone—someone who wasn't there, someone she didn't even remember but felt like she should.

She used to lie in bed, staring at the ceiling, wondering if there was a piece of herself missing.

If there had ever been a time when she belonged somewhere.

To someone.

But now, there is no reaching.

No searching for an answer that won't come.

Only this moment.

Only her.

She breathes deeply, the steam from her tea rising in slow, curling tendrils.

She thinks about how far she has come.

How waking up used to feel like a fight—a battle against the emptiness, against the silence.

How she used to wish for a different kind of morning.
One filled with voices.
One filled with footsteps other than her own.
One filled with something more.
But she doesn't wish for that anymore.
She doesn't need that anymore.
Because this morning—this moment—is hers.
And it is enough.

She moves through her apartment, her fingertips trailing along the worn edges of her furniture, the soft fabric of the couch, the cool surface of the kitchen counter.

Everything in this space is hers.

Every choice, every object, every breath she takes.

She picks up one of the notes she left the night before, the ink still dark, the words steady.

"You are enough."

She smiles.

Not because she needs the reminder today—

But because she believes it.

For the first time, she truly believes it.

She takes her time getting ready, letting the morning unfold without urgency.

She brushes her hair slowly, feeling the weight of it against her shoulders.

She picks out a dress she hasn't worn in months, just because she wants to.

She applies lipstick—not for anyone else, not to impress, not to be seen—

Just because it makes her feel alive.

She steps back, looking at her reflection in the mirror.

And for the first time, she doesn't look for something missing.

She doesn't search for a shadow of someone she used to be.

She just sees herself.

And she likes what she sees.

She decides to go out.

Not because she has to.

Not because she feels lonely.

But because the world is out there, and she wants to exist in it.

On her terms.

She walks through the city streets, feeling the pulse of life around her.

She watches couples holding hands, families laughing, friends lost in conversation.

And she doesn't feel envious.

She doesn't feel out of place.

Because she is here.

And she belongs—not to anyone else, but to herself.

She stops at a café she has never been to before.

Orders a coffee.

Finds a table by the window and lets herself exist in the moment.

She writes in her notebook, not because she is lonely, but because she loves putting her thoughts onto paper.

She watches the world move and doesn't feel like an outsider.

She feels like she is exactly where she is meant to be.

Alone.

But never lonely.

Just free.

That night, as she slips into bed, she doesn't feel the emptiness that used to keep her awake.

She doesn't feel like she is waiting for something, for someone.

She doesn't feel like she is missing a part of herself.

She just feels whole.

She runs her fingers over the note under her pillow, the same one she has left there for days now.

"You are not alone. You never were."

And for the first time, she truly believes it.

She smiles to herself, letting her eyes drift shut.

Tomorrow, she will wake up alone again.

But that is not a tragedy.

It is a gift.

Because she has herself.

And that is enough.

The night air presses against the window as she lies in bed, listening to the hum of the world outside. The city never truly sleeps—cars whisper down the roads, distant voices drift through open balconies, and somewhere, the faint melody of a song plays through a neighbor's speaker.

She likes this sound.

It reminds her that she is not the only one awake, though she is alone.

But being alone no longer feels like something to endure.

It feels like something she has chosen.

She turns onto her side, staring at the ceiling.

Once, the quiet used to feel unbearable.

She would toss and turn, waiting for something to fill the silence—a memory, a voice, anything.

But now, the silence is hers.

A companion.

A reassurance.

She doesn't fight it anymore.

She breathes it in, lets it wrap around her like a familiar song.

There is peace in this.

In knowing she has herself.

In knowing she is enough.

The next morning, the sky is the color of soft peaches and golden honey when she wakes up.

She stretches, feeling the warmth of her own body against the sheets.

There is no urgency.

No alarms demanding her attention.

No hurried footsteps outside her door.

Just the gentle rhythm of her own breathing.

The steady beating of her heart.

The knowledge that she is here.

And that is enough.

She takes her time getting out of bed, savoring the way the sunlight filters through the curtains, painting golden streaks across the wooden floor.

She makes her morning coffee with slow, deliberate movements, watching the steam curl and dance in the morning air.

She enjoys the first sip, closing her eyes as the warmth spreads through her.

This is her moment.

Her ritual.

No one else's.

Just hers.

Today, she decides to do something new.

Not because she is trying to distract herself.

Not because she needs to prove anything.

But simply because she wants to.

She steps into her closet and pulls out a dress she hasn't worn in years.

A soft, flowing fabric in the color of deep wine, with delicate lace at the edges.

She remembers buying it once, long ago, telling herself she would wear it for a special occasion.

But that occasion never came.

She was always waiting.

For the right time.

For the right person.

For the right reason.

But today, she doesn't need a reason.

Today is the occasion.

She stands in front of the mirror, letting her fingers trace over the fabric.

For a moment, a strange feeling flutters through her.

A whisper of something familiar.

Like she has worn this before.

Like she has stood in front of a mirror just like this, adjusting the lace, smoothing the folds, waiting for someone to knock on the door and tell her she looks beautiful.

The thought lingers, like the fading echoes of a dream.

She blinks, and it's gone.

She shakes her head, brushes it off.

She is used to these strange, fleeting thoughts.

They come and go like waves on the shore, touching her for a moment before retreating, leaving only emptiness behind.

She doesn't dwell on them anymore.

She has taught herself not to.

She steps outside, the fresh air wrapping around her like a gentle embrace.

She walks without a destination, letting the world unfold before her, moment by moment.

She notices things she never used to before.

The way the sunlight flickers through the gaps in the trees.

The way laughter spills from a café, warm and unrestrained.

The way a little girl tugs on her mother's hand, pointing at something with unfiltered joy.

She watches them, but she does not ache.

Not anymore.

She simply observes.

Simply exists.

And that is enough.

She finds herself in a bookstore, fingers running along the spines of books she has never read.

She picks one at random, flipping through the pages, letting the scent of ink and paper fill her lungs.

She buys it without thinking twice.

A gift to herself.

Because she deserves it.

Because she doesn't need an excuse to do something kind for herself.

Because she is enough, and she always will be.

That night, she sits on her balcony, book in hand, a cup of tea resting beside her.

The city stretches out before her, lights blinking like tiny stars.

She breathes in deeply, feeling the weight of the day settle in her bones—not as exhaustion, but as contentment.

She doesn't miss anyone.

She doesn't wish for a different life.

She doesn't long for something she cannot name.

For the first time, she feels complete.

Whole.

Not because she found someone to fill the empty spaces inside her.

But because she has realized—there were never any empty spaces to begin with.

She was whole all along.

She just had to see it.

As she closes her eyes, letting sleep pull her under, she knows—

Tomorrow, she will wake up alone again.

But it will not be lonely.

It will be freedom.

And freedom is the most beautiful love she has ever known.

IX

The Music of Solitude

The first sound she hears is the soft rustling of the wind against her window.

It's quiet.

Still.

But within the silence, there is a rhythm.

A beat that belongs only to her.

She wakes up slowly, stretching beneath the warm sheets.

There's no rush.

No schedule.

No one waiting for her, expecting anything from her.

And she loves it.

She rolls onto her back, staring at the ceiling, feeling the steady thump of her own heartbeat.

The only music she has ever truly needed.

She moves through the morning with ease, humming to herself as she makes her coffee.

A tune without words, just something soft and familiar.
She doesn't know where she learned it—
It feels like something from long ago, something buried deep in her bones.
But she doesn't question it.
She simply lets it be.
She hums as she pours her coffee.
Hums as she steps onto the balcony, letting the morning sun paint golden streaks across her skin.
Hums as she watches the city come alive beneath her, people rushing to places they need to be.
She doesn't need to be anywhere but here.
She closes her eyes and lets the music inside her chest rise.
She sways to it, moving her head lightly to the beat of her own existence.
No one is watching.
No one is listening.
But she dances anyway.
It starts with a small movement.
A gentle rocking of her hips, a tapping of her fingers against the railing.
And then—
She spins.
A slow, effortless twirl, her bare feet brushing against the wooden floor.
And suddenly, she is dancing.
With no music but the wind.
No rhythm but her heartbeat.
No audience but the sky.
And for the first time in a long time—
She feels alive.

She moves through the apartment, the soft fabric of her dress swirling around her.

She dances in the kitchen, twirling between the cabinets.

She dances in the living room, letting her laughter slip out in breathless, carefree gasps.

She dances in front of the mirror, watching her reflection move—wild and free, untamed by the weight of expectations.

She lifts her arms, reaching toward something she cannot name.

She doesn't need a partner.

She doesn't need an audience.

She doesn't need a reason.

The music is inside her.

It has always been inside her.

She stops for a moment, breathless, her heart pounding.

A thought slips into her mind, soft but persistent.

"Have I done this before?"

Something about the way her body moves—

The way her feet know exactly where to step—

The way she feels at home in the rhythm—

It feels like memory.

Like she has done this a thousand times before.

Like she used to dance, not just for herself—

But for someone.

The thought lingers, stretching across her mind like a song on the edge of fading.

But she doesn't chase it.

She doesn't let it take away from this moment.

She is here.

She is dancing.

And that is enough.

She collapses onto the couch, laughing softly to herself.

She feels light.

Like she has shaken off the dust of a past she cannot remember.

Like she has stepped into a version of herself she was always meant to be.

She reaches for her notebook, flipping to a fresh page.

Her fingers tremble slightly as she writes, her handwriting steady, deliberate.

"I danced today. I felt like I had done it before. Maybe I have. But it doesn't matter. I am happy. And that is enough."

She closes the notebook, pressing it to her chest.

The music is still there, thrumming beneath her ribs.

Soft.

Steady.

Hers.

Tomorrow, she will wake up alone again.

And she will dance again.

Because she doesn't need a stage.

She doesn't need an audience.

She doesn't need anyone.

She has herself.

She has the music inside her.

And that is all she has ever needed.

She stays on the couch for a long time, her chest rising and falling in steady breaths, her fingertips tingling from the rush of movement.

There is something so utterly beautiful about this moment—this perfect solitude wrapped around her like an old, familiar embrace.

The silence is not empty.

It hums with the echo of her own laughter.

It holds the rhythm of her heartbeat.

She tilts her head back against the cushion, staring at the ceiling, the faintest hint of a smile still playing at the edges of her lips.

How many people get to feel this free?

How many people dance just because they can?

A breeze drifts in through the open window, carrying with it the distant sounds of the city—a car honking, a street performer playing the violin, the laughter of children somewhere far below.

And then—

A song.

It's faint, barely there, but it reaches her like a whisper from another life.

She sits up, heart beating a little faster.

The melody is familiar.

Too familiar.

She doesn't know where she's heard it before, but something about it makes her feel—

Cold.

Not in a way that is unpleasant.

But in a way that feels like stepping into the shadow of a memory she cannot name.

She rises from the couch, drawn toward the window as if something beyond the glass is calling her.

The song drifts in again, carried by the wind, slipping through the spaces between her ribs.

It is soft.

Melancholic.

It makes her think of warmth and belonging, of something just out of reach.

And yet—

She is alone.

She has always been alone.

Hasn't she?

Her fingers tighten around the window frame as she listens.

Something flickers in the depths of her mind—

A glimpse of hands reaching for hers.

Laughter twirling through the air like golden dust.

A voice—soft, warm, calling her name—

Her name.

Her name.

She frowns.

That doesn't make sense.

She shakes her head, as if shaking off the weight of something unseen.

This is ridiculous.

She has never belonged to anyone.

She has never needed to.

She steps away from the window, closing it gently, shutting out the song.

She tells herself she's just imagining things.

Just another trick of solitude.

The mind plays games when left unchecked for too long.

She has read about it.

People start seeing things that aren't there.

Hearing voices in the wind.

Longing for things that never existed.

She won't let that happen to her.

She won't allow it.

And yet—

As she moves through the apartment, picking up the book she had started the night before, her fingers feel unsteady.

She tells herself she is fine.

That nothing is wrong.

That she has spent years building a life that doesn't need anyone else in it.

But the song lingers.

Faint and ghostlike.

Curling around the edges of her thoughts, refusing to let go.

And for the first time in a long time—

She wonders if she is truly alone.

Or if she has only been made to forget.

The song stays with her long after she shuts the window.

It lingers in the quiet corners of her mind, slipping through the cracks of her thoughts when she least expects it.

Soft.

Familiar.

Unshakable.

She curls up on the couch, pulling her knees to her chest, her book resting against her lap. But the words blur together, the sentences refusing to settle in her mind.

All she can hear is that song.

All she can feel is that strange, unsettling pull toward something she cannot name.

She shuts the book, pressing her hands against her temples.

"Stop thinking about it."

But it's impossible.

Because the more she tells herself to forget, the more she wonders—

What if she already has?

She rises to her feet, pacing the apartment.

Her hands brush against the bookshelves, the furniture, the paintings on the walls.

Everything here is hers.

Every item, every memory, every moment—
All carefully built, carefully chosen.
This is her world.
A world where she belongs to no one but herself.
So why does she feel like something is missing?
Why does she feel like the song was not just a song—
But a piece of something she once knew?
She stops in front of the small wooden chest in the corner of the room.
She hardly ever touches it.
It holds old things—things she has told herself don't matter anymore.
Little trinkets, notebooks half-filled with poetry, letters she once wrote to herself on lonely nights.
She kneels before it, fingers hovering over the latch.
She hesitates.
There is no reason to do this.
She is fine.
She doesn't need to go looking for ghosts.
But her hands move on their own, pushing open the lid, the scent of aged paper and faded ink rising to meet her.
She sifts through the contents slowly, carefully.
Old journals.
A dried flower she doesn't remember keeping.
A stack of photographs—
Wait.
Photographs?
Her breath catches as she lifts them.
She never keeps photographs.
She has never kept photographs.
She has no one to remember.
Her life has always been hers alone.
So why—

Why is she in these pictures?

And who are the people standing beside her?

She stares, heart pounding, as she flips through the photos.

A younger version of herself, laughing.

Arms wrapped around people she does not know.

A warm light in her eyes—one she has never seen in her reflection before.

There is a man in one of the pictures, his arm draped casually over her shoulder, his smile familiar in a way that makes her chest ache.

A woman, holding her hand, their fingers intertwined.

Children.

Faces blurred with time, but their presence undeniable.

She grips the edges of the photographs, her vision swimming.

"No."

This doesn't make sense.

This isn't real.

She knows her life.

She knows who she is.

She has always been alone.

She has always been alone.

Right?

Her hands tremble as she presses the photos against her lap.

For the first time in years, something feels wrong.

There is a gap inside her, one she has never noticed before—

Or one she was never meant to notice.

Her breathing turns shallow, her pulse hammering against her ribs.

She tries to tell herself this is nothing.

That the photographs must belong to someone else.
That this is some kind of mistake.
But deep down—
Deep, deep down—
She knows.
She knows.
This song in her mind.
These faces in her hands.
This ache in her heart.
She has not been living alone.
She has been made to forget that she wasn't.
She squeezes her eyes shut, pressing a hand against her forehead.
She doesn't want this.
She doesn't want to question.
She has built a life she loves.
A life of peace, of solitude, of freedom.
She has never needed anyone.
So why does she feel like she has lost everyone?
The song plays again.
Soft.
Familiar.
Unshakable.
And this time, she listens.
This time, she lets it take her back.
And what she finds waiting in the depths of her mind—
Changes everything.

X

A Table for One

She arrives at the restaurant just as the sun begins its descent, casting a golden glow across the city streets. The familiar scent of fresh bread and roasted spices drifts through the air as she steps inside, the warmth of the place wrapping around her like a quiet embrace.

The hostess smiles at her, a polite, practiced expression.

"Table for one?"

She nods.

She has always loved this moment—this quiet reassurance that she belongs to no one but herself.

A table for one.

A meal for one.

A life for one.

And it is enough.

She follows the hostess to a small corner table by the window, where the city stretches out before her. People move in hurried steps outside—couples hand in hand, friends laughing, families lost in easy conversations.

She watches them with a quiet kind of fondness, not envy.

She does not wish for what they have.

She has her own version of happiness, one that is not tied to another person's presence.

She loves eating alone.

She loves the freedom of ordering whatever she wants, of not having to make small talk between bites, of being fully present with her own thoughts.

She loves the silence.

And yet—

Something feels off tonight.

The waiter approaches, pen poised, ready to take her order.

"Would you like to start with something to drink?"

She looks down at the menu, scanning the options.

And then—

Her breath catches.

Her fingers tighten around the menu, the words blurring slightly.

Because there, in the middle of the list, is something that makes her heart skip a beat.

"Winter Rose Tea."

She doesn't know why it affects her.

She doesn't even remember ever trying it.

And yet, something in her chest knows this drink.

Knows it deeply.

She can almost taste it—something floral and warm, something that lingers long after the last sip.

"Miss?" the waiter prompts gently.

She swallows, shaking off the unease.

"I'll have the Winter Rose Tea," she says before she can stop herself.

As the waiter nods and walks away, she exhales slowly, pressing her hands against her lap.

She doesn't understand why she ordered it.

Why she felt something at the sight of it.

But as she sits there, alone at her table, something shifts in her.

Something unsettles.

The tea arrives in a delicate porcelain cup, steam curling into the air like whispers of a forgotten past.

She stares at it for a long moment.

Then, carefully, she lifts the cup to her lips and takes a sip.

And suddenly—

The restaurant fades away.

She is somewhere else.

The taste is familiar.

Too familiar.

Like a ghost of a memory buried deep beneath the life she has convinced herself she knows.

Laughter echoes in her mind—soft, warm, real.

"You always steal my tea."

A voice.

A voice she knows.

But she doesn't know how she knows it.

She gasps, the porcelain cup clattering against the saucer as she sets it down, her hands shaking.

Her breath comes fast, uneven.

The memory vanishes as quickly as it came, slipping through her fingers like mist.

She grips the edge of the table, struggling to steady herself.

This isn't possible.

This isn't real.

She is alone.

She has always been alone.

Hasn't she?

The restaurant continues around her, unaware of the storm unraveling inside her.

She forces herself to take slow, measured breaths, to push the strange moment aside.

It doesn't matter.

She is here.

She is alone.

And that is enough.

So she picks up her fork.

She eats her meal.

She finishes her tea, even though every sip feels like swallowing a ghost.

She pays the bill.

She leaves the restaurant.

And she tells herself that nothing has changed.

But deep inside—

She knows something has cracked.

And there is no going back.

She steps out of the restaurant, the night air cool against her skin, but there is a warmth curling inside her—a warmth that is not comforting.

It is the heat of confusion.

The unsettling burn of something slipping through the cracks of her mind.

She walks down the street, her fingers brushing absentmindedly against her wrist, where a faint mark lingers—something that looks almost like an old scar, but she doesn't remember how she got it.

Or maybe she does.

Maybe she did.

But she has forgotten.

She moves through the streets with careful steps, the lights of the city flickering around her.

The distant sound of a violin plays from a street corner, mingling with the hum of passing cars, the murmur of conversations she is not a part of.

She has always loved this feeling—

The in-between of things.

The quiet space where she exists alone, untethered to anyone.

But tonight, something in her feels unmoored.

She stops in front of a small bakery, its warm glow spilling onto the pavement.

Through the glass, she watches a man behind the counter, laughing as he hands a cupcake to a little girl who beams up at him with pure joy.

There is something about the moment that grips her chest.

Something achingly familiar.

A flicker of warmth against the edges of her mind.

For a second, she sees something else—

Hands covered in flour.

Laughter filling a tiny kitchen.

A voice—teasing, soft, safe.

"You always get icing on your nose."

The memory is so vivid that she takes a step back, her breath catching in her throat.

The warmth.

The laughter.

The voice.

It is real.

But it shouldn't be.

Because she has never had that.

She has never baked with someone.

She has never laughed like that, felt like that.

Has she?

She turns away from the bakery quickly, pulling her coat tighter around her.

This is ridiculous.

This is just her mind playing tricks on her.

Maybe she's read too many books, absorbed too many stories of people who have someone.

Maybe the loneliness is finally catching up to her, trying to rewrite her past, trying to make her believe that she once belonged to something bigger than herself.

But she won't let it.

She won't.

She takes a deep breath and keeps walking.

She is alone.

She has always been alone.

She has never needed anyone.

And yet—

The memories come anyway.

She reaches home and locks the door behind her, pressing her back against it.

Silence greets her, stretching across the empty apartment like a familiar song.

She exhales slowly, forcing herself to relax.

Everything is fine.

Everything is normal.

She moves through her evening routine—taking a shower, changing into comfortable clothes, making herself a cup of chamomile tea.

She sits by the window, staring at the night sky.

She tells herself she is okay.

That this feeling will pass.

But as she lifts the cup to her lips, the taste sends another jolt through her.

Not because it is unfamiliar.

But because it is not.

"You always take your tea with too much honey."

A voice in her head, warm with amusement.

Her fingers tighten around the cup.

She never puts honey in her tea.

She doesn't even like it sweet.

But her hands—

Her hands move before she can think.

She looks down at the honey jar on the table, its lid slightly askew.

As if she had reached for it without realizing.

As if—

She had done this before.

A thousand times.

For someone else.

Or—

For herself.

Because once, a long time ago—

She had been someone else.

Her breath trembles as she sets the cup down.

She looks around the apartment—the bookshelves, the walls, the paintings she chose with such care.

Everything here is hers.

Everything here is a life she built alone.

So why does she feel like a stranger in it?

Why does she feel like she is standing in the ruins of something she has already lost?

She closes her eyes.

Tries to push it all away.

But the memories don't stop.

They press against the edges of her mind, persistent, demanding.

Not full memories—

Not yet.

Just pieces.

Flickers of warmth.

Echoes of laughter.

The lingering touch of someone's hand against hers.

She has spent years loving her solitude.

She has spent years knowing she is enough.

But tonight—

For the first time—

She wonders if she has been loving a life that was never meant to be hers.

The cup of tea sits untouched on the table, its surface still, unbroken—unlike the storm unraveling inside her.

She runs a hand through her hair, breathing in, breathing out. Steady, steady. But the air feels heavier now, thick with something unspoken, something forgotten.

She should just go to bed. Sleep would clear her mind, reset her thoughts.

But she doesn't move.

Because the apartment suddenly feels too small, the walls pressing in like whispers she can't quite hear.

She glances at the bookshelves, at the little trinkets she has collected over the years. Each item should be a marker of her life, a piece of her journey.

But right now—

They look unfamiliar.

Like they belong to someone else.

Or maybe—

Like they belong to a version of her that she has somehow misplaced.

She pushes back her chair and stands abruptly, her pulse uneven.

Enough.

She strides to the bedroom, flicks off the light, and buries herself under the covers.

Sleep.

That's all she needs.

Tomorrow, this unsettling feeling will fade.

Tomorrow, she will wake up and remember who she is.

But sleep does not come easily.

She tosses and turns, shifting between wakefulness and something deeper—something darker.

And in that fragile space between dreams and reality, the memories start creeping in again.

A warm kitchen, the scent of freshly baked bread filling the air.

Soft hands adjusting the collar of her dress before school.

Laughter at the dinner table, voices overlapping, teasing, loving.

"You always sit in that chair."

The voice is gentle, affectionate.

She looks up—

But the face is blurred, slipping away the moment she reaches for it.

Her heart races.

The memory is so real.

But it shouldn't be.

She has never sat at a dinner table like that.

She has never had a family fussing over her.

She has never—

She jolts awake, a sharp gasp breaking the silence of the room.

Darkness engulfs her, the only sound her ragged breathing.

She presses a hand to her chest, feeling the wild rhythm of her heartbeat.

It was a dream.

Just a dream.

But the ghost of it lingers, refusing to fade.

Her eyes dart toward the nightstand, where a small notebook rests.

She doesn't even remember buying it.

But somehow, it is there.

She hesitates before reaching for it, fingers grazing the soft, worn edges of the cover.

Slowly, she flips it open.

And there—

On the very first page—

Is her own handwriting.

"Don't forget who you are."

Her breath catches.

Her vision blurs.

She flips the pages frantically, her fingers shaking.

More words. More messages.

"You are not alone."

"You belong somewhere."

"Remember."

She slams the notebook shut, her chest heaving.

What is this?

What is this?

She presses her hands to her temples, trying to steady herself.

She has always been alone.

She has always loved being alone.

Hasn't she?

Hasn't she?
But something in her refuses to let this go.
Something in her is breaking.
She picks up the notebook again, staring at those words.
"Remember."
And for the first time—
She is terrified of what she might find.

XI

The Mirror Reflects Her Only Companion

The morning light spills through the curtains, casting long shadows across the room. It's quiet. Too quiet.

She sits up slowly, her body heavy with the weight of a restless night.

The notebook still lies on the nightstand, its presence feeling louder than it should.

She doesn't touch it.

Not yet.

Instead, she swings her legs over the side of the bed and makes her way to the bathroom. The cold tiles press against her bare feet as she steps inside, closing the door behind her.

She turns on the tap, splashing water onto her face, hoping to wash away the lingering unease.

And then—

She looks up.

And sees herself.

The mirror is large, spanning nearly the entire wall. It reflects everything—the dark circles beneath her eyes, the crease between her brows, the quiet exhaustion settling into her bones.

She studies herself carefully.

She has always been her only witness.

The only one to see her joy, her sadness, her resilience.

She does not have someone to hold her and tell her that she is enough.

So she does it herself.

"You are strong."

The words are barely above a whisper.

"You are complete."

Her voice is steady. Resolute.

But the reflection does not seem convinced.

She leans in closer, watching the way her eyes shift, the way uncertainty flickers beneath them.

She has spent years building this life, brick by brick, shaping it into something she loves.

A life without anyone else.

A life where she is enough.

Then why—

Why does she feel like something is missing?

Her fingers tighten around the sink.

She won't do this.

She won't undo everything she has built.

She is not someone who longs for things she does not have.

She is not someone who aches for ghosts of memories she does not remember.

She is not—

Her gaze drops.

And she freezes.

There, at the base of her throat, is a faint, almost invisible scar.

She doesn't remember how she got it.

She doesn't remember ever having it.

But it's there.

Real.

Undeniable.

Her breath catches.

The mirror reflects her, and only her.

But suddenly—

She is no longer sure that's the whole truth.

Because if she is enough—if she has always been enough—

Then why does it feel like there was once something more?

Something she has lost?

And why—

Why does it feel like the mirror knows?

Her breath slows, but her pulse does not.

She reaches up, fingertips brushing the scar at the base of her throat.

It is smooth. Almost faded.

Yet, beneath the touch, it burns.

Not physically. Not in a way she can explain.

But in a way that feels wrong.

Like something hidden beneath her skin is trying to claw its way out.

She exhales sharply and looks back into the mirror.

Her reflection stares at her—steady, silent, unwavering.

For years, it has been her only companion.

She has whispered to it in the dead of night.

She has smiled at it, reassured it, told it that they—she—is enough.

And it has always agreed.

Until now.

Her fingers trail down to the bathroom counter, gripping the cool marble as she studies herself more closely.

She tilts her head, letting the morning light highlight her features.

The same face she has always known.

The same face she has woken up to every single day.

Then why does it look...different?

Why does it feel like she is staring at a stranger?

She tries to shake the thought away, forcing a small smile.

"You are enough," she says again, softer this time.

A reassurance.

A promise.

Her lips curve, but the reflection does not look convinced.

The longer she stares, the more she feels it—

Something beneath the surface.

Something she cannot see but can feel.

Like standing in an empty house and sensing that it was once filled with voices.

Like reading a book and realizing that whole chapters are missing.

Like looking at her own face and knowing, somewhere deep inside, that it is not the whole story.

Her hand moves before she can think, opening the drawer beneath the sink.

Inside, neat and organized, are small belongings—skincare, hair ties, a brush.

Normal things. Familiar things.

But then—
Something else.
A small wooden box, tucked into the back corner.
She doesn't remember putting it there.
She doesn't even recognize it.
But her hands do.
Because the moment she touches it, something inside her shifts.
Something clicks.
She swallows, slowly pulling the box out and setting it on the counter.
Her fingers tremble as she lifts the lid.
Inside, there are only a few things.
A folded piece of paper.
A silver ring.
And a photograph.
Her breath stutters.
She reaches for the photograph first, unfolding it carefully.
And then—
Her world tilts.
It is her.
Younger. Maybe by a few years.
Smiling.
But she is not alone.
Beside her, arms wrapped around her shoulders, is a boy.
Or a man.
His face is bright, blurred slightly at the edges from time or wear.
But his smile—
His smile feels like something she once knew by heart.
She grips the counter, staring at the image as something inside her breaks.

This is impossible.

This is not her life.

She has always been alone.

She has always loved being alone.

Then why does this photo exist?

Why does it feel like a lie to tell herself she was never held like that?

Never loved like that?

Her head spins.

She looks down at the silver ring, resting at the bottom of the box.

Simple.

Delicate.

Familiar.

She picks it up, holding it between her fingers.

It fits perfectly on her hand.

Her stomach twists.

How?

Why?

What is this?

She forces herself to unfold the last piece of paper.

And in her own handwriting, the words stare back at her:

"Don't forget him."

The room tilts.

She grips the counter to steady herself, but nothing feels real anymore.

Her own reflection blurs in the mirror, as if it, too, is no longer sure who she is.

A sickening thought slams into her.

She has spent years standing in front of this mirror.

Telling herself she is enough.

That she has always been alone.

That she has always loved it this way.

But what if—

What if she has been lying to herself all this time?

What if she wasn't supposed to be alone?

What if—

She had someone?

What if she lost them?

What if the mirror has never been her only companion—

But simply the only one left?

The paper trembles in her hands.

"Don't forget him."

The words stare back at her, sharp, cutting through the very foundation of her existence.

She doesn't remember writing them.

She doesn't remember him.

She has spent years building this life, crafting a world in which she is self-sufficient, in which she needs no one, in which she is whole on her own.

So why does it feel like the ground beneath her is breaking apart?

She grips the bathroom counter, her knuckles turning white.

"This isn't real," she whispers, shaking her head.

It's a misunderstanding. A mistake.

The photo—the ring—the words—

They do not belong to her.

She has always been alone.

Hasn't she?

Hasn't she?

But the photograph in her hands says otherwise.

The boy in the image—his arm around her, his laughter frozen in time—feels too familiar.

She forces herself to examine his face.

His dark, kind eyes.

The way he leans into her, like it's the most natural thing in the world.

Like he belongs there.

Like she belonged to him.

Her pulse pounds in her ears.

A memory tugs at the edges of her mind—fragile, distant, like a whisper she can't quite hear.

Fingers intertwined.

A voice, warm and teasing.

"You always overthink everything. Just breathe, okay?"

She gasps.

The moment shatters before she can grasp it fully.

She stumbles back from the sink, her back hitting the wall.

Her breath comes in sharp, uneven bursts.

She can't do this.

She won't do this.

With trembling hands, she shoves the photograph back into the wooden box, snapping the lid shut.

She grips the edge of the sink, forcing herself to look up again—

At her reflection.

She expects to see herself. The same woman who has spent years telling herself she is enough.

But instead—

She sees something else.

An emptiness.

A crack in the foundation.

A hollowness she has never noticed before.

It's as if she has been looking at her reflection her whole life, believing it was whole—only to now realize it was just a fragment.

A half-truth.

A lie.

"No," she whispers.

She shakes her head, gripping the counter as if it could anchor her.

"I am enough."

The words feel weaker this time.

"I have always been alone."

Her reflection does not respond.

Her own eyes—her only companion—no longer believe her.

And that terrifies her more than anything else ever has.

She stares at herself, at the hollow reflection in the mirror.

Her own eyes seem foreign.

Wide. Uncertain. Afraid.

She was never afraid before.

She was never uncertain.

She had built a world for herself where she was whole, where she was enough, where solitude was her choice—not a consequence.

But now—

Now, that world feels like a carefully constructed illusion.

A house of cards, toppling with the weight of one photograph, one piece of paper, one forgotten scar.

Her fingers twitch.

She wants to rip the photograph apart.

To burn the note.

To erase the doubts clawing at her mind, threatening to unravel everything she knows about herself.

Because if she acknowledges this—if she admits that there is something missing—

Then she has to ask why.

And she isn't sure she's ready for the answer.

She grips the wooden box tightly, pressing it to her chest.

It feels heavier than it should.

Not because of its weight, but because of what it holds.

It is proof.

Proof that she is not who she thought she was.

Proof that there was once someone else in her life.

Someone she has forgotten.

Or someone she has been forced to forget.

Her breath hitches.

A sharp, electric pain shoots through her skull.

She gasps, stumbling back, her body curling inward as if to shield itself from an unseen force.

A pressure builds behind her temples, distant but unbearable—like a scream echoing through her mind, but muffled, unreachable.

She squeezes her eyes shut.

Flashes.

Fragments.

A voice.

"You won't lose me."

The pain intensifies, cutting through her like a blade.

She cries out, clutching her head as the world spins, bends, blurs.

Her knees give out.

The box slips from her grasp, hitting the floor with a soft thud.

The lid flies open.

The photograph lands face-up beside her.

And through the haze of pain, through the storm tearing through her mind—

She hears it.

A laugh.

His laugh.

A sound she once knew.

A sound she once loved.

A sound she should not have forgotten.

Her eyes snap open, heart pounding, breath ragged.

And as she stares at the photograph, at the boy beside her past self, a realization crashes into her—

This wasn't just someone she lost.

This was someone who was erased.

XII

When the World Goes Silent

The world has always been quiet for her.

No buzzing phone.

No missed calls.

No one asking, Where are you? or Are you okay?

For years, this silence has been her sanctuary—a space where she is free from expectations, from obligations, from the weight of belonging to someone else.

A space where she belongs only to herself.

And she loves it.

At least, she thought she did.

Morning unfolds like it always does.

She wakes up to the soft hum of the ceiling fan, to the sound of birds outside her window.

She does not wake up to messages or missed calls.

Her phone is exactly as she left it—face down, undisturbed, untouched by anyone but her.

No notifications flash across the screen.

No unread messages from people who care.

Because there are no people who care.

There never have been.

She stretches, relishing the stillness of the morning.

This is how she likes it.

No obligations.

No one asking for her time, her attention, her love.

She belongs to no one.

She is free.

And yet—

Beneath that freedom, beneath the comfortable silence—

Something feels off.

She makes coffee, sitting by the window as she watches the city come to life.

Cars pass, people hurry along the sidewalks, lovers hold hands, families laugh over breakfast.

The world is full of connections.

But none of them belong to her.

She used to find peace in this—watching from a distance, untouched by the messiness of relationships.

But today, she notices something different.

She notices the way people check their phones.

The way their faces light up at a message.

The way they smile at the sound of a familiar voice.

She watches a woman on the opposite balcony, laughing into her phone as she cradles a cup of coffee.

A man passing by on the street, holding a little girl's hand, talking to someone on a call.

A teenager grinning down at her phone, fingers moving fast as she types.

She watches them.

She watches the way their lives are intertwined.

And suddenly, the silence around her feels...louder.

She picks up her own phone.

Blank screen.

No messages.

No missed calls.

Nothing.

She doesn't know why she expected anything different.

Why would there be messages?

Who would text her?

Who would call?

She has always been alone.

She has always loved it this way.

So why does her chest feel hollow?

Why does the silence feel so crushing today?

She locks the phone and tosses it onto the couch.

She refuses to let herself feel this.

She is not lonely.

She is free.

She has told herself this a thousand times.

And she will tell herself a thousand more if she has to.

She forces herself into her routine.

A long shower, washing away the thoughts that threaten to linger.

A clean outfit—comfortable, effortless, as if today is just like any other.

She steps out, towel drying her hair, and walks past the mirror without looking.

She doesn't want to see herself today.

She doesn't want to meet her own eyes and see doubt.

She doesn't want to ask the question she is afraid of.

"What if I wasn't always alone?"

"What if I was supposed to have someone?"

No.

No.

She shakes her head, gripping the towel tighter.

She won't do this.

Not today.

Not ever.

The day stretches on, empty but full of distractions.

She cleans, rearranges furniture, dusts off shelves she hasn't touched in months.

She plays music, loud enough to drown out the silence.

She pretends she doesn't keep glancing at her phone.

She doesn't know what she's waiting for.

Nothing is coming.

No one is reaching out.

No one is remembering her.

But—

That's good.

That's how she wants it.

That's how it has always been.

Right?

Right?

By evening, she feels restless.

The world outside moves on.

People meet.

People talk.

People exist together.

She used to find comfort in the idea that she wasn't a part of it.

That she was separate.

That she was different.

But now, she isn't so sure.

She finds herself aching for something she can't name.

A presence she can't remember.

A voice she should remember.

She tries to push it away.

She tells herself she loves this life.

But tonight, when she curls up in bed, when she turns off the lights and lets the quiet settle in—

She listens to the silence.

And for the first time in years, she hates it.

The silence is unbearable.

She lies in bed, eyes open, staring at the ceiling. The darkness wraps around her like a second skin, heavy and suffocating.

Her room is quiet. Too quiet.

The city outside hums with distant life—faint honks of cars, the occasional bark of a stray dog, the murmur of voices drifting from open windows. But none of it reaches her.

None of it belongs to her.

She shifts onto her side, her fingers brushing the empty pillow beside her.

The spot is cold. It has always been cold.

Because she has always been alone.

Hasn't she?

Hasn't she?

She squeezes her eyes shut, inhaling deeply, willing herself to believe it.

To believe that this silence is hers.

That she chose this.

That this is the life she wanted.

That this is freedom.

But the words feel hollow tonight.

And for the first time, she wonders—

Has she been lying to herself all along?

She wakes up unrested.

The silence lingers like a ghost, pressing against her ribs as she moves through the motions of the morning.

She makes coffee, but it doesn't taste right.

She plays music, but it doesn't drown out the emptiness.

She scrolls through her phone, her fingers hovering over her contacts list—staring at names that feel meaningless.

No one would care if she disappeared.

Would they?

Would anyone even notice?

She slams her phone down.

She won't think about this.

Not today.

Not ever.

She goes outside.

She tells herself she just wants fresh air, but deep down, she knows.

She is searching.

For something.

For someone.

But she doesn't know who.

She doesn't know what she is missing—only that there is a gaping hole inside her, an absence that has always been there, hidden beneath layers of denial.

She walks through the park, past mothers with their children, past lovers sharing quiet conversations, past groups of friends laughing over old stories.

She tells herself she doesn't envy them.

That she doesn't need them.

But the ache in her chest says otherwise.

She sits on a bench, watching the world move around her.

And for the first time, she wonders—

Did she ever belong to someone?

Was there a time when she wasn't just watching from the outside?

The thought haunts her.

She returns home, restless, unsettled.

The silence feels louder now, stretching through the walls, pressing against her skin.

She turns on the TV.

She blasts music.

She talks to herself, just to fill the void.

But nothing helps.

Because the emptiness isn't in the room.

It's inside her.

She opens drawers she hasn't touched in years.

She rifles through old books, old clothes, old things that should feel familiar but don't.

Then she finds it.

A wooden box, tucked away in the corner of her closet.

She doesn't remember putting it there.

She doesn't remember owning it.

Her fingers hesitate.

A cold dread creeps into her veins.

She doesn't know why, but something tells her—

If she opens this box, if she looks inside—

Everything will change.

She swallows, her heartbeat hammering against her ribs.

She lifts the lid.

And there, lying at the bottom—

Is a photograph.

The air leaves her lungs.

Her hands tremble as she picks it up, bringing it closer.

A boy.

A boy with dark, familiar eyes.

A boy with an arm around her.

A boy who looks at her like she is his whole world.

She gasps, nearly dropping the picture.

Her stomach twists, a sharp, painful lurch.

She doesn't recognize him.

But something deep inside her does.

The silence around her is no longer comforting.

It is terrifying.

Because in this moment, she realizes—

She hasn't been alone all her life.

She just forgot.

Or worse—

Someone made her forget.

Her breath is ragged now.

Her pulse pounds in her ears.

She flips the photograph over, hoping for a name, a date, a clue—

And scrawled in unfamiliar handwriting, there are only three words.

"Don't forget him."

Her vision blurs.

Her grip tightens on the photograph, as if letting go would mean losing him all over again.

And for the first time in years, the silence isn't empty.

It is filled with the echoes of something lost.

Something stolen.

Something she is determined to find.

The photograph shakes in her grip.

"Don't forget him."

The words stare back at her, taunting, whispering, pressing against her skull like a distant voice she should recognize—but doesn't.

Her heart races.

Her breathing is uneven, shallow, like she's forgotten how to inhale properly.

Who is he?

Who wrote this?

And more importantly—

Why does she feel like she already knows the answer?

Her fingers tighten around the edges of the photograph as a deep, throbbing pressure builds inside her head.

Like something buried—something suppressed—is fighting to resurface.

She squeezes her eyes shut.

Think.

Think.

Think.

But the memories won't come.

They hover at the edge of her mind, like static on an old radio, blurry and unreachable.

She knows there is something she isn't remembering.

But why?

Why is her mind a locked door, and who took the key?

She stumbles backward, dropping the photograph onto the floor.

The room feels smaller now.

The walls press in, the silence thick and suffocating.

This isn't right.

This isn't her.

She is happy.

She is whole.

She loves her life.

She chose this life.

Didn't she?

Didn't she?

A deep, aching doubt claws its way into her chest.

What if she was wrong?

What if she wasn't always alone?

What if she had people—people who loved her, who laughed with her, who called her name—

And she forgot them?

Or worse—

They forgot her.

Her stomach twists violently at the thought.

The idea of being erased, of being invisible, of being a ghost in people's memories—

It terrifies her.

She shakes her head, pressing her palms against her temples.

No.

She won't do this to herself.

Not now.

Not again.

She bends down, carefully picking up the photograph, her fingers tracing the boy's face.

There's something familiar about the way he smiles.

Something warm.

Something safe.

But she doesn't know why.

And that—

That makes her want to scream.

She forces herself to move.

She needs answers.

And she won't find them standing here, drowning in silence.

Her hands shake as she pulls out the wooden box, searching through its contents.

More photographs.

More memories that don't belong to her.

She flips through them, one by one.
A beach.
A birthday cake.
A school uniform.
A messy handwriting on the back of a note—"Don't be late again, sleepyhead."
Her breath catches.
She reads the words again.
And again.
And again.
A blurry image flashes in her mind—
A voice, teasing and familiar.
"If you're late one more time, I swear—"
Her head throbs.
Her vision darkens.
The memory slips away before she can grasp it.
Gone.
Just like the boy.
Just like her past.
Her chest tightens, her fingers curling into a fist around the paper.
This isn't right.
This isn't fair.
Someone took something from her.
Someone made her forget.
And she—
She wants it back.
The silence around her is no longer comforting.
It is a lie.
For years, she thought she was alone.
She thought she had no one.
She thought she was happy.
But now—

Now, she knows better.
She wasn't just alone.
She was made to be alone.
She was forced to forget.
And whoever did this—
Whoever erased her from their world—
She will find them.
She will make them remember.
She will make them tell her the truth.
No more silence.
No more pretending.
No more forgetting.
She grips the photograph, her knuckles white.
And for the first time in years, she lets herself whisper the words—
"Who am I really?"

XIII

The Night Sky Is Enough

The night air is cool against her skin.

She steps onto the balcony, the city stretching out below her—silent, still, unaware of the storm inside her.

The photograph remains clutched in her hand.

Her fingers have traced its edges so many times now that they feel like part of her.

She should be sleeping.

She should be resting.

But sleep won't come.

Not after what she found.

Not after the emptiness in her chest turned into something raw, something broken, something aching for answers.

She lifts her gaze.

The sky is clear tonight.

The stars are scattered across the darkness like whispers of something eternal, something untouched by time or memory.

She exhales, slow and steady.

At least the stars have never left her.

At least the sky has never forgotten her.

She leans against the railing, the weight of the photograph pressing into her palm.

A boy she doesn't remember.

A life she might have lived.

A truth she isn't sure she's ready to face.

Her throat tightens.

She has spent so long telling herself that she is enough.

That solitude is a choice.

That she is whole, even without anyone beside her.

But tonight, she isn't sure.

Tonight, she wonders if she ever truly believed it—

Or if she simply had no other choice.

She tilts her head back, watching the stars.

How many times has she done this?

How many nights has she stood here, whispering secrets to the sky, waiting for an answer that never came?

The universe has always listened, even when no one else did.

But tonight, she isn't looking for comfort.

She is looking for proof that she exists.

That she matters.

That she isn't just a forgotten name in a forgotten story.

She closes her eyes.

In the darkness behind her lids, she tries to remember.

Not just the boy.

Not just the words scrawled in the past.

But something—anything—that proves she wasn't always alone.

A touch.

A voice.

A single moment where she was held, where she belonged.

But all she sees is the vastness of space.

The endless, stretching night.

And the stars blinking back at her, as if whispering—

"We remember you."

A lump rises in her throat.

She presses her hand against her chest, feeling the steady beat beneath her ribs.

She is here.

She is real.

She exists.

Even if the world has forgotten her.

Even if she has forgotten herself.

She opens her eyes, blinking back the tears that threaten to spill.

Maybe she doesn't have answers yet.

Maybe the truth is buried deep, waiting to be unearthed.

But for now, she has the stars.

She has the night.

She has the quiet understanding that no matter what happens, no matter who remembers her or who doesn't—

The sky will always be enough.

And that, for tonight, will have to be enough, too.

The night is endless.

She grips the iron railing of her balcony, staring at the stars, feeling the quiet hum of the universe pressing into her chest.

The sky—so vast, so eternal—feels like the only thing that truly knows her.

It has seen every version of her.

The girl who danced barefoot in the rain.

The girl who sat alone on rooftops, tracing constellations with her fingertips.

The girl who thought she was complete in her solitude.

The girl who now realizes that somewhere, somehow—she has been erased.

The photograph is still in her hand.

Her fingers are numb from holding it too tightly, as if letting go would mean losing a piece of herself all over again.

She should feel something more.

Shock.

Panic.

Fear.

But all she feels is emptiness.

A quiet, aching numbness that stretches across her ribs, curling into the spaces of her lungs, making it hard to breathe.

She presses her forehead against the cool iron railing, inhaling deeply.

The stars don't ask questions.

They don't demand answers.

They simply exist.

And tonight, that is enough.

A gust of wind brushes against her skin, carrying with it the scent of the city—distant rain, warm earth, and something faintly familiar.

For a split second, it feels like a memory trying to return.

A voice in the wind.

A laugh that doesn't belong to her.

A name she can't quite grasp.

It's there—just there—at the edge of her consciousness.

And then—

It's gone.

Just like everything else.

She squeezes her eyes shut, frustration curling in her stomach.

What kind of person forgets a life they once had?

What kind of person loses themselves so completely?

Her grip on the railing tightens.

She has always loved her life.

She has always found peace in her solitude.

But now, an unfamiliar fear creeps into her thoughts—

Has she been loving a life that was never meant to be hers?

The stars blink back at her, quiet and understanding.

They are the only constant in her existence.

They have seen her on the nights she laughed for no reason, arms outstretched, spinning beneath their glow.

They have seen her on the nights she cried into the silence, pretending it didn't hurt.

They have seen her on the nights she pretended not to care.

And now—

They see her on this night, standing on the edge of something she doesn't understand, holding onto a piece of her past with shaking hands.

She exhales, slow and deliberate.

It doesn't matter.

If she has lost everything—if everyone has forgotten her—then at least the night sky remains.

The universe remembers her, even if no one else does.

And tonight, that will have to be enough.

Even if the ache in her chest tells her otherwise.

Even if, deep down, she is terrified that she is truly, completely alone.

A whisper of a thought lingers in her mind as she turns to go back inside.

A small, fragile question that refuses to fade.

What if the stars aren't the only ones who remember me?

What if there's someone else?

The thought terrifies her.

And yet—

It is the only thing that makes her heart race with something other than fear.

Hope.

She doesn't know if she's ready.

She doesn't know if she will ever be.

But tomorrow—

Tomorrow, she will start looking.

For the truth.

For herself.

For the life that once belonged to her.

And for whoever it is that she was never supposed to forget.

The night stretches infinitely before her, vast and untouched, just like the silence in her life.

She watches the stars flicker in the distance, tiny flames suspended in the dark.

It's funny, she thinks, how something so far away can feel so close.

The stars are her only witnesses.

They have seen her wake up to empty rooms.

They have seen her celebrate her own victories in whispers, her own birthdays in candlelight with no voices singing along.

They have seen her hold onto solitude like a fragile treasure—

Because if she lets go, if she reaches for something more—

What if there is nothing there?

She sighs, tilting her head back, the photograph still clutched in her trembling fingers.

There is an unsettling weight in her chest tonight, heavier than the usual loneliness, heavier than the silence she once welcomed.

Tonight, she cannot shake the feeling that something has been stolen from her.

Not just memories.

Not just people.

But herself.

A life that once belonged to her but now feels unreachable, like a faded dream.

She thought she was happy.

She thought she was whole.

But tonight, staring at the night sky, she wonders—

What if she was simply made to forget?

She runs her fingers over the rough edges of the photograph, her pulse steady but her heart anything but.

She should go inside.

She should leave the past where it belongs.

But something in her won't let her move.

A whisper in the wind, a voice she cannot place—

"Look closer."

She blinks, her breath hitching.

For a brief moment, she swears she hears someone say her name.

Not just in her head.

Not just in her thoughts.

But in the world, somewhere beyond the walls of her loneliness.

Somewhere real.
She spins around, scanning the empty streets below.
Nothing.
The city sleeps.
The world is silent.
It was nothing.
Wasn't it?
Or has she spent so long in solitude that she has begun to hear echoes of what she has lost?

Her fingers curl around the railing, her knuckles white.
She cannot keep living in questions.
She cannot keep pretending that this silence is enough.
Because the truth is—
It isn't.
It never was.
And the worst part?
Maybe it never will be again.
She exhales, slow and controlled, grounding herself in the weight of her body, in the cold iron beneath her hands, in the rhythm of her own breathing.
She looks back up at the sky.
The stars still glow, steady and patient.
They have never forgotten her.
But for the first time in years—
She is terrified that someone else has.
And for the first time, she is ready to find out who.
Tomorrow.
Tomorrow, she will start looking.
Even if she doesn't know where to begin.
Even if she is afraid of what she might find.
Because something inside her whispers—
She wasn't always alone.
And she is done believing the lie that she was.

XIV

The Art of Coming Home to Herself

The morning sun filters through her window, casting a soft golden glow across the room.

She lies still, eyes open, staring at the ceiling as if the answers she seeks might be written in the cracks above her.

Something feels different today.

The silence is the same.

The emptiness of her home is the same.

But she is not.

Something inside her has shifted, like the quiet unraveling of a thread she didn't even know was holding her together.

She turns her head, her gaze landing on the photograph she left on the nightstand.

A boy she doesn't remember.

A past she might have forgotten.

A life she isn't sure ever belonged to her.

And yet, for all the uncertainty, one thing is clear—

She is done pretending.

Done pretending she has always been alone.

Done pretending that her solitude is her choice.

Done pretending that the empty spaces in her life are simply things she never needed.

Because what if she did?

What if she still does?

She pushes back the covers and sits up, letting the cool air wrap around her skin.

For years, she has lived with a sense of purpose that no one else could define.

She has created her own happiness, built a world that belongs only to her.

She has filled her days with routines she loves—long walks, quiet mornings, coffee brewed just the way she likes it.

She has told herself, again and again, that this life is enough.

That she is enough.

But now, with the weight of doubt pressing against her ribs, she wonders—

Was she building a life for herself, or was she simply surviving in the ruins of one she forgot?

She stands, moving through her home with careful steps, as if the walls might whisper secrets to her if she listens closely enough.

The familiar comfort of her apartment feels different now, as though she is seeing it for the first time.

Every object, every carefully placed book, every framed painting—

Are they hers?

Or did someone once stand here beside her, choosing them with her?

She walks into the kitchen, running her fingers along the smooth surface of the counter.

How many meals has she made for one?

How many nights has she eaten in silence, believing she was the only one who ever belonged here?

She has loved this life.

She still does.

But love and loneliness are not opposites.

And for the first time, she wonders if she has spent all these years loving a life that was never meant to be lived alone.

She takes a deep breath and turns toward the door.

She doesn't know where she's going.

She doesn't even know who she is looking for.

But for the first time, she is stepping into the world not just as someone who loves her solitude—

But as someone who is willing to remember.

And no matter what she finds—

She knows one thing.

She is not losing herself.

She is coming home to herself.

Even if "home" is not what she thought it was.

She lingers at the doorway, her fingers resting on the cold metal of the handle.

For years, this apartment has been her sanctuary.

A world crafted by her own hands, untouched by anyone else's presence.

A life of her own design.

Every chair, every book, every photograph on the wall—everything here was chosen by her.

At least, that's what she has always believed.

But belief and truth are not the same.

And now, as she stands on the edge of something she cannot name, she is forced to ask herself—

What if I did not build this life?

What if I simply woke up in it one day and made it my own because I had no other choice?

The thought unsettles her, pressing against her ribs like something fragile and sharp.

She lets go of the handle and turns back, her gaze sweeping across the apartment as if seeing it for the first time.

It is beautiful, in a quiet, understated way.

The bookshelves are filled with well-worn pages, each spine carefully aligned.

The windows are framed by sheer white curtains that sway gently with the breeze.

The walls hold paintings of landscapes she has never seen in person, and yet she feels drawn to them, as if they are fragments of something she once knew.

It is hers.

It has always been hers.

And yet—

Why does it feel like it was once meant for more than just one person?

She walks over to the small wooden desk near the window, trailing her fingers over its surface.

This is where she writes her thoughts.

Where she leaves herself notes, small reminders that she is enough.

But tonight, she wonders—

Has she been writing to herself all this time?

Or has she been writing to someone else, someone she no longer remembers?

She picks up one of the many notes scattered across the desk, the handwriting undoubtedly her own.

"You are strong. You are whole. You are not missing anything."

She swallows hard, her fingers tightening around the paper.

Not missing anything.

She has told herself that for years.

But now, standing here with an unfamiliar ache curling in her chest, she isn't so sure.

The floor creaks as she moves toward the bookshelf, drawn to a stack of journals tucked away in the corner.

She keeps them for herself—records of her days, her thoughts, the small joys she collects like delicate treasures.

She pulls one out, flipping through the pages, watching her own words blur in front of her.

There is something unsettling about them now.

She has always written with certainty.

With clarity.

But as she skims through the entries, something gnaws at the edges of her mind.

Not a memory.

Not yet.

But a feeling.

Like reading a story she has written—

Only to realize she is not the main character.

Her heart pounds as she turns to the last entry, written just days ago.

"I have always loved my life."

"I have never needed anyone to complete me."

"I do not know if I was ever meant to be alone, but I have made peace with it."

She exhales shakily, pressing the journal to her chest.

Peace.

That is what she has been telling herself.

But tonight, as she stands in the middle of her quiet, carefully built life, she feels anything but at peace.

She feels like a girl standing in the remnants of a home that once held more than just her presence.

She feels like a girl who has spent years writing letters to herself—

Because no one else was there to do it.

She feels like a girl who has spent so long convincing herself that she is enough—

That she never stopped to ask if she was also missing something.

Or someone.

The thought makes her chest tighten, fear and something dangerously close to hope stirring inside her.

She is afraid.

Afraid of what she might find if she dares to search for the missing pieces.

Afraid of what it will mean if she learns that she was never truly alone.

But she is also ready.

Ready to step beyond the walls she has built around herself.

Ready to open the door and walk out into a world that might hold the answers she never thought to ask for.

Ready to come home to herself—

Even if home is something she has yet to remember.

She exhales, setting the journal down carefully, as if it might shatter under the weight of the truth she has only just begun to grasp.

And then, with steady hands and a heart that is both terrified and determined, she turns back to the door.

She reaches for the handle.

She doesn't know where she is going.

She doesn't know if anyone is waiting for her.

But tomorrow—

Tomorrow, she will start searching.

For the truth.

For the past.

For herself.

And no matter what she finds, she knows one thing—

She has spent years convincing herself that she has everything she needs.

Now, she is ready to find out if that was ever true.

She hesitates at the door, her fingers resting lightly on the handle.

How many times has she stood here, looking out at the world, only to turn back?

How many times has she convinced herself that she needed nothing outside of these walls?

She has built a life that belongs to her.

She has spent years loving her solitude, finding beauty in being enough for herself.

She is strong.

She is whole.

She has everything she needs.

Hasn't she?

Her breath is unsteady as she lets go of the handle and steps back, retreating into the safety of the familiar.

She moves through her home slowly, touching the things that make up her world—

The books, the paintings, the carefully placed notes she leaves for herself.

Each one is a piece of the life she has built.

A life she swore was enough.

But tonight, for the first time in years, she wonders—

Did I build this life because I wanted to?

Or because I had no other choice?

The thought unsettles her, sinking into her bones like a truth she has spent too long avoiding.

She wants to believe she has always been content in her solitude.

But now, she isn't sure if she was ever meant to be alone at all.

She picks up a framed photograph from her nightstand.

It is the same one she found days ago—the one with the boy she does not recognize.

She stares at it, tracing the edges with her fingertips.

He is smiling, his eyes alight with something familiar, something warm.

And yet, she does not remember him.

She does not remember the moment this picture was taken.

She does not remember who she was when it was.

A dull ache presses against her temples, and she shuts her eyes.

For years, she has convinced herself that her past does not matter.

That all she needs is this present, this life she has built from the ground up.

But now, she is not so sure.

Now, she wonders if the past has been waiting for her all along.

She sets the photograph down carefully and walks to her desk.

Her journals are stacked neatly, their pages filled with thoughts, dreams, and reassurances she has written to herself over the years.

She picks up the one on top and flips through it, skimming the words she has read so many times before.

"You are enough."

"You are whole."

"You do not need anyone to complete you."

The words feel different now, heavier somehow.

She has written these things to herself for years.

But tonight, as she reads them, she feels something new creeping in—

Doubt.

Was she writing these words to believe them?

Or was she writing them to forget something else?

The thought sends a shiver down her spine.

She grips the journal tighter, turning to the last page, searching for answers.

Instead, she finds something she doesn't remember writing.

A single sentence, written in shaky, uneven handwriting—

"If I am enough, why does it feel like something is missing?"

Her breath catches in her throat.

She stares at the words, her heart pounding.

She has no memory of writing this.

And yet, the ink is hers.

The handwriting is hers.

The doubt is hers.

She closes the journal slowly, pressing it against her chest as the weight of realization settles over her.

For the first time, she cannot ignore the feeling that has been haunting her for weeks—

She is not just missing people.

She is missing pieces of herself.

She lets out a slow breath, steadying herself.

Then, with a newfound resolve, she places the journal back on the desk and turns toward the door once more.

She is afraid.

Afraid of what she might find.

Afraid of what she might remember.

But fear has kept her inside for too long.

And now, for the first time, she is ready to step beyond these walls and search for what was lost.

Even if she doesn't know where to begin.

Even if the truth terrifies her.

Because no matter what she finds—

She knows she cannot keep pretending that this life is enough when her own words betray her.

She cannot keep pretending she was always meant to be alone.

She takes a deep breath, her fingers tightening around the handle.

Then, with steady hands and an unsteady heart—

She turns the knob.

And steps outside.

The air outside is different.

It is colder than she remembers.

Or maybe she simply never noticed before.

She stands still, just beyond the doorway, the night stretching out before her. The city hums in the distance, a faint glow of streetlights casting long shadows across the pavement.

She has stepped outside countless times before. To buy groceries. To take long evening walks. To exist among people without truly being a part of them.

But tonight is different.

Tonight, she is not just stepping out.

She is searching.

For something she cannot name.

For something she is terrified to find.

She moves forward, each step uncertain yet deliberate.

There is nowhere specific she plans to go.

And yet, her feet seem to know the way.

She walks past familiar streets, past the café she has sat in alone so many times, past the bookstore where she has spent hours losing herself in stories that are not hers.

Everything is the same.

And yet, something about tonight feels different.

Like the world is watching her.

Like it has been waiting for her to remember something she has spent too long forgetting.

She stops in front of a quiet park, the kind most people pass by without a second glance.

The trees sway gently, their leaves whispering secrets she cannot hear.

She doesn't know why she came here.

She doesn't know why her heart is racing.

But something in her gut tells her—

She has been here before.

Not yesterday.

Not last week.

But before.

Before she became the woman who loved being alone.

Before she convinced herself that she needed no one.

Before she forgot.

The thought is like a needle to her skin, a small prick of awareness that spreads like wildfire.

She steps forward, her breath shallow as she scans the park.

Empty swings sway in the breeze.

A streetlight flickers.

The benches are vacant—except for one.

She nearly turns away.

Nearly dismisses it as another empty memory, another place that holds no meaning.

But then—

She sees it.

A book.

A single, worn-out book resting on the bench.

Waiting.

She swallows hard, her body moving before her mind can catch up.

Her hands tremble as she picks it up, feeling the weight of something unfamiliar yet familiar in her grip.

She turns it over, her pulse hammering in her ears.

The cover is faded.

The edges are frayed.

And inside—

Inside, there is handwriting.

Not a stranger's.

Hers.

Her own handwriting, messy and hurried, filling the first page with words she does not remember writing.

"If I ever forget, I hope I find my way back to this."

Her stomach twists.

Her head pounds.

She flips through the pages, frantic now, her breathing uneven.

More words.

More of her words.

Pages and pages of things she does not remember—

Dates.

Names.

Memories.

The truth, buried in ink.

And then, at the very end—

A note.

One sentence.

One last, undeniable truth.

"You were never alone. You just forgot."

Her breath leaves her in a silent gasp.

The book slips from her hands.

And suddenly, everything she has ever known feels like a lie.

She stumbles back, gripping the bench for support.

Her heart is beating too fast.

Her chest is too tight.

The world tilts.

She closes her eyes, trying to breathe, trying to understand.

She had a life before this.

A family.

People.

Memories.

But they are gone.

Not because they left.

Not because she chose solitude.

But because she forgot them.

Or worse—

They forgot her.

The realization crashes over her like a wave, cold and unforgiving.

Her entire life—this life—was built on an illusion.

She was never truly alone.

She just convinced herself she was.

Because it was easier than facing the truth.

A sob rises in her throat, but she swallows it down.
She is not ready to break.
Not yet.
Not until she finds out why.
Why she forgot.
Why her life became this.
Why her own memories erased her from the people who once loved her.
She grips the book, holding it close like a lifeline.
She doesn't know where to go next.
She doesn't know who she will find.
But she knows one thing—
She is done pretending.
She is done convincing herself that this is enough.
Because she had a life before.
And now, she is going to get it back.
No matter what it takes.

XV

The Love That Stays Forever

She walks home in silence, her hands gripping the book as if it holds the last piece of herself.

The night presses in around her, cold and endless, but she does not shiver.

Her mind is too loud.

Too full.

Too restless.

She had spent years telling herself she was alone. That she had no one, and that was enough.

But now, as the truth cracks through her carefully built walls, she realizes—

She had lied to herself.

Not because she wanted to.

Not because she enjoyed solitude.

But because something—someone—had made her forget.

And yet, despite this new, terrifying truth, one thing remains unchanged.

Her love for life.

Even in loneliness, she loved her life.

Even when the world was silent, she found beauty in it.

And now, even as she pieces together the truth, she knows—

She will always choose herself.

She reaches her doorstep but does not go inside immediately.

Instead, she looks up at the sky.

The stars are scattered across the darkness, quiet witnesses to everything she has ever been.

How many nights has she stood here, speaking to them, believing they were the only ones who listened?

How many times has she whispered into the wind, convincing herself that she did not need anyone else to hear her?

But what if someone once did?

What if there were voices that once called her name—before she forgot them?

Her fingers tighten around the book.

She doesn't have all the answers yet.

She doesn't even know where to begin looking.

But she knows one thing—

Even if the world has forgotten her, even if the people she once loved are gone, she will never stop loving the life she has.

Because love is not just in people.

It is in the way the wind brushes against her skin.

It is in the sunrises she wakes up early to watch.

It is in the books she reads, the music she listens to, the small joys she creates for herself.

It is in the quiet, in the solitude, in the moments when she is simply alive.

Love is not just who stays.

Love is what remains, even when everything else is gone.

And her love for life—

That will stay forever.

No one can erase that.

Not even the past.

Not even the truth.

She smiles, just slightly, as she finally steps inside.

The search for answers can wait until morning.

Tonight, she will let herself rest in the one thing that has never left her.

Her love for life.

Because in the end, no matter what happens, no matter what she finds—

She will always have that.

She closes the door behind her, leaning against it as if she needs the support. The house is just as she left it—quiet, still, untouched by the weight of the truth pressing down on her.

Her gaze drifts across the room, taking in the small details of her life.

The lone teacup sitting on the kitchen counter, remnants of the chamomile tea she made earlier.

The blanket draped over the couch, slightly wrinkled from when she curled up with a book.

The soft hum of the wind slipping through the slightly open window.

It's all the same.

And yet—

Everything feels different.

She moves slowly, walking toward the mirror in the hallway.

It stands tall, its frame old but sturdy, reflecting a woman who is no longer sure of who she is.

For years, she thought she knew.

She was the woman who needed no one.

The woman who found joy in solitude.

The woman who was whole all on her own.

But was that really the truth?

Or just the only story she had left?

She lifts a hand, tracing her fingers along the glass, watching her reflection do the same.

Her eyes are steady, but somewhere in their depths, there is uncertainty.

She once believed she could see everything in her own gaze—strength, independence, unwavering contentment.

But now, she wonders—

What is missing?

She turns away, unable to look at herself any longer.

The book she found sits on the table, waiting.

She hesitates before reaching for it, as if touching it again will unravel everything she has tried so hard to hold together.

But the truth is already unraveling.

She already knows—she was never truly alone.

And the more she lets that realization sink in, the more her heart aches with a loss she cannot fully remember.

She sits down, flipping through the pages once more.

Her handwriting is there, familiar and foreign all at once.

Dates she does not recall writing.

Memories that feel like echoes of a life she cannot grasp.

And the final words, the ones that shattered everything she thought she knew—

"You were never alone. You just forgot."

Her fingers tremble over the ink.

Who wrote these words?

Who did she forget?

And why?

The questions weigh heavy on her chest, but beneath them, there is something else.

Something deeper.

A realization that makes her close the book, pressing it against her heart as she exhales shakily.

No matter what she uncovers, no matter what she remembers—

Her love for life remains.

It always has.

Even in the emptiness, she found beauty.

Even in the loneliness, she found peace.

Even in the silence, she found music.

That love—her love—was never a lie.

It was real.

It was hers.

And nothing, not even forgotten memories or missing people, can take that away from her.

The clock on the wall ticks softly, marking the passing time.

She could spend hours searching for answers tonight.

She could chase after the past until morning.

But she doesn't.

Because tonight—

She chooses the present.

She chooses the warmth of her own existence.

She chooses herself.

Again.

Always.

She stands, walking toward the window, pushing it open a little wider.

The night breeze rushes in, cool against her skin, wrapping around her like an old friend.

She closes her eyes and smiles.

Not because she has found all the answers.

Not because she is whole just yet.

But because, in this moment, she is still here.

Still breathing.

Still loving the life she has, even as the past whispers through the cracks.

And no matter what comes next—

That love will stay forever.

Because it is hers.

And no one—not even the universe—can take it away.

She stands by the window for a long time, watching the city breathe.

Lights flicker in the distance. A car hums down the empty street. Somewhere, far away, laughter spills into the air—soft, fleeting, gone before she can grasp it.

She wonders if she has ever been in that laughter.

If she has ever stood beneath streetlights with someone beside her, smiling, talking, belonging.

The thought lingers, an ache in the quiet.

She could ignore it.

She could close the window, shut out the world, and return to the life she knows best—the one where she is enough, where she doesn't need anyone.

But for the first time, that thought doesn't bring comfort.

It brings questions.

It brings doubt.

It brings the terrifying possibility that all these years, she has been loving a life that wasn't hers to begin with.

And yet, even as the uncertainty seeps in, she knows—

Her love for this life is real.

It has always been real.

Because even if she forgot the people, even if she lost the memories, she never lost the love she carried for the small things.

For the way sunlight filters through her window in the morning.

For the sound of rain tapping against the glass.

For the books stacked by her bedside, waiting for her hands to turn their pages.

For the simple joy of a quiet cup of tea.

For the way her feet know the rhythm of the earth when she walks, as if she is part of it, as if she belongs.

Even if she has lost people, she has never lost this.

And that means something.

That means everything.

She turns away from the window, walking back toward the book on the table.

Her fingers skim the edges of the worn pages.

There is so much she doesn't understand yet.

So much she doesn't remember.

But instead of rushing to uncover the truth, instead of letting panic take hold, she breathes.

Deep, steady, present.

The past can wait for her.

Tonight, she is here.

With herself.

With the life she has loved—even when it wasn't whole.

And that love?

That will stay forever.

Even when memories fade.

Even when the truth unravels.

Even when she is no longer the same person she was before.

Because love is not just about who we have.

It's about what we hold onto, even when everything else is lost.

And she—

She will always hold onto this.

No matter what happens next.

She picks up the book, pressing it to her chest one last time before setting it aside.

Tomorrow, she will search for answers.

Tomorrow, she will begin the journey to reclaim the pieces of herself that time stole.

But tonight?

Tonight, she simply exists.

And for now—

That is enough.

That is everything.

Because love, the kind that truly matters, never leaves.

And hers?

Hers has never wavered.

Hers will stay forever.

About The Author

KALPITHA R

Kalpitha R is a passionate storyteller and the author of Bloom of Becoming, a heartfelt journey of self-discovery and transformation. Currently in 10th grade, she balances academics with her love for writing, dance, and music—each a reflection of her emotions and creativity.

From a young age, Kalpitha has been captivated by the power of storytelling. For her, writing is more than just words on a page—it is a way to express emotions, capture fleeting moments, and bring to life the unspoken thoughts that reside in the heart. Whether through the graceful movements of dance or the melodies of music, she finds inspiration in every rhythm and every beat of life.

Her stories often explore themes of resilience, identity, and human connections, aiming to touch the hearts of readers and make them feel seen and understood. She believes that every story carries a heartbeat of its own, waiting to be felt by those who need it most.

With a deep love for nature and the world around her, Kalpitha continues to draw inspiration from her surroundings, pouring her thoughts and emotions into stories that she hopes will stay with readers long after the final page is turned.

She dreams of writing books that leave an impact, stories that comfort, inspire, and remind people that they are never alone in their journeys.

A Note From The Author

There is beauty in solitude, in loving the life you build for yourself. But sometimes, hidden in the quiet spaces, there are truths waiting to be remembered.

If this book has spoken to you in any way, I hope it reminds you that no matter where you are in life—whether surrounded by love or standing on your own—you are enough. You always have been.

I would love to hear your thoughts! Connect with me and share your reflections. Your words mean the world to me.

Coming Next: The Life She Lost

She thought she had no one. She thought she was alone by choice.

But the past never truly disappears. And neither do the people we once called ours.

As memories begin to return, so does the life she never knew she lost.

Her story isn't over yet.